HER FAVOR

HART SISTERS: BOOK TWO

ALIE GARNETT

Edited by Thoth Editing

Image © DepositPhotos – nd3000

Cover Design © Designed With Grace

❀ Created with Vellum

For my R.

CHAPTER 1

Evangelina Hart Singleton hated funerals. Maybe it had to do with burying her father and her husband before she turned twenty-five. Maybe it was because she hated crying in public and funerals always made her cry.

Bill Reed had been her neighbor her entire life, and she considered him a grandfather, since she had lost both of her own too soon to really remember them. He had been one of her dearest friends, and since her father had died, had also taken on the role of mentor. Though they had different philosophies on what farming entailed, they still liked to bounce ideas off each other. He was a row crop farmer beginning to end, and she catered to the farmer's markets in the area. She helped him at harvest and planting, and he helped her whenever she needed an extra hand. She was going to miss the old man.

The body beside her started to squirm, and she laid a hand on his knee. Ben's twitching stopped immediately. Her son was eleven now and not too happy about missing a day of school to attend a funeral. It seemed funerals were even worse than school. Bill had been one of the major influences in his life and had been there for Ben ever since he'd lost his own father at one and his grandfather at six.

Evie wished she could have sat next to Betty, Bill's wife. The woman had been a rock for Evie during her own husband and father's passing and she wanted to be there for the older woman. But Betty was seated between her two grandchildren, Clementine and Jasper. Twelve-year-old Clementine was Ben's best friend but her grandson, Jasper Reed, was already an adult. Neither of Betty's two sons had bothered to show up for their father's funeral, but neither had bothered to do much of anything ever, including raise their respective children. They had left that up to their aging parents.

Evie glanced at the man beside her, he was easy on the eyes. Or at least that's what her sister Zoey had said when she saw him yesterday for the first time in years. Evie wasn't at the farm when Jasper made it home from Minneapolis where he worked as some kind of accountant. Even Evie's older sister Della had commented on how Jasper had grown up nicely.

Both comments made her laugh as Evie had been aware of his eye candy status for years. Neither of her sisters had really been around for years, Zoey had just gotten out of the Army this last spring and even though Della had worked as a lawyer in Minneapolis for years, she'd never run into the neighbor boy there. But Evie had been here watching him grow into a man. What she didn't tell her sisters was that she couldn't count how many times she had seen him shirtless when they were both helping his grandfather. That was a sight to be seen.

Harmless fun, as he was five years her junior and probably saw her as another annoying adult back then. At least a year younger than her sister, he and Zoey had buddied around growing up like Ben and Clementine now did. So for Evie, he had always been something nice to look at, nothing more.

Ben started wiggling again. Tapping her hand with a hopeful look, he pointed to the pew behind them containing her sisters, Della and Zoey, and Zoey's fiancé, Gabe Watson. Nodding in agreement, her son moved one row back, away from his stern mother, she assumed. As much as she tried not to overanalyze it, it seemed the closer he got to being a teenager the less he liked to spend time with his mother.

Focusing on the flower arrangement on the casket, she smiled sadly. They were actually not flowers, they were wheat stocks from Bill's own fields. Bill would have loved that his flowers were wheat.

A light tug on her scalp had her leaning forward just enough that her long hair let free of it entrapment behind her back. The sensation was unusual, she always wore it in a braid to get it out of the way and off her face. But today she had thought it would be nice to be able to hide behind the long, blond locks, in case she couldn't control the tears. She hated funerals.

Slowly she swept her hair from behind her and let it rest over her shoulder to block her view of Jasper. She had to get her mind off his warm body squeezed next to hers in the small pew. She felt his leg nudge hers a little, so she looked down. To her embarrassment, she discovered that her hair was covering his leg and his hands resting on his lap. Quickly she pulled her hair the other direction and off Jasper's suit pants. Her sister's comments on how he filled out a suit nicely was making her act crazy, she thought.

Since Ben had moved Evie worried that she was sitting a little to close. She scooted away from his warm body, and for some reason felt she was now alone in the church full of people. She tried to focus again on the minster's words about one of her dearest friends, but it was impossible. Jasper's leg had started to bounce like Ben's just a few minutes before. Without thinking, she reached over and took his hand in hers and rested it on his leg. At her touch the bouncing stopped, instantly. Just like Ben's had. But unlike Ben, Jasper didn't let go of her hand.

After a few minutes of holding his hand she felt him shift, but as she was bringing her hand back to her lap, he grabbed it again. But this time instead of lightly holding it over his, he intertwined their fingers. Which felt much more intimate. Now she couldn't concentrate on the words coming from the minister's mouth because all she could hear was her heart beating loudly in her ears. *Relax, woman,* she chided herself, *you cannot go crazy just because a man is touching you. You're in a church.*

Calming herself as best she could, she went back to staring at the wheat stocks on the casket. She had cut them this morning for Grandma Betty; they had stood not far from the house Betty and Bill had shared for forty years. Tomorrow she and Zoey would have to get back in Bill's combine and harvest the rest of the wheat. Bill would be pissed at himself for dying in the middle of harvest. There were still at least two days of harvesting before the wheat was done, then in a little over a month it would be corn. Bill hated to leave things undone.

A rogue tear escaped her eyes as she tried to concentrate on something else. She hated crying in public. Hated it. Jasper squeezed her hand and she felt his thumb graze her leg and she slid her eyes in his direction. His other hand was holding out a tissue for her. She took it and dabbed her eyes with it not wanting to mess up the makeup that she had so carefully applied today. Another rare thing for Evie Singleton, makeup.

She shifted with resolve to stop crying and stop thinking about Jasper. The Jasper part got harder when he shifted their hands so the back of his was pressed against her leg. There was a thin layer of cotton from her dress between his hand and her thigh, but she felt the heat of his hand just the same. The jolt of electricity made her breath catch in her throat. He shifted a little and the back of her hand was now resting against his leg. Their intertwined hands were sandwiched on the pew between their legs.

With resolve, Evie decided to enjoy the warmth that was spreading through her body while it lasted. In an hour, it would be over, and everything would go back to normal. He would go back to Minneapolis and she would be here in Birch Cove. He would be a swinging bachelor and she would be his grandma's widow neighbor, again. The thought depressed her today. She hated funerals.

She also blamed her little sister Zoey for this. Zoey made being in love look fun. Zoey made everything look fun. Zoey was the most fun person Evie had ever met, and she had practically raised the girl. She glanced back at her red-haired baby sister, who was currently holding her boyfriend's hand who had his arm around her. Zoey noticed her looking at them and smiled at her, sadly. Evie smiled back at the happy couple then turned back to the front. After seeing Zoey all comforted, she wanted Jasper to put his arm around her.

Not Jasper. Not Jasper. Not Jasper, Evie reminded herself. Jasper was the boy next door who used to mow her lawn when Ben was a baby. Used to throw rotten vegetables at her until she threw them back at him. Used to never wear a shirt if it got over ninety degrees. Used to be one of Zoey's best friends. Now he was a nice-looking man with excellent hand holding skills.

Stop, she commanded her mind. He was twenty-five years old and thought of her as a middle-aged widow. Nothing more. He probably didn't even know she was only thirty. She knew that when she had her thirtieth birthday people had thought that she was closer to thirty-five. Maybe it had only been one person, but wasn't that enough?

Sighing, she listened to the minister finish and then the funeral director walked up and closed the casket. Jasper squeezed her hand, and she squeezed his back. As the casket was wheeled away she let herself lean into him a little as the tears started again. She felt his thumb rub against her leg, up and down, as if in comfort. Shouldn't she be comforting him? Bill was his grandfather. Feeling she had let him down a little, she should be better at this. She hated funerals.

With one final squeeze, Jasper dropped her hand as he stood and she followed. He turned to her and handed her another tissue. Now she had tears running down her cheek. Clementine and Betty walked down the row of pews, then Jasper started to leave and she followed. When he got to the end of the pew, he stopped. He turned her way and nodded for her to go before him. Surprised at the move her eyes snapped to his, trying to indicate he should go first, but he didn't move. Knowing people were watching she hurriedly she wiped her eyes one more time and stepped out in front of him.

Now she had to face all her family and friends obviously crying, without Jasper walking in front of her to hide her tears with his large body. Had she mentioned how much she hated funerals?

Suddenly she felt Jasper's warm hand on her back, her bare back, thanks to the low dip in her blue dress, as he ushered her down the pews. A calm settled over her and she suddenly felt better about facing all these people with tears in her eyes. He was such a nice guy.

When they were past the last pew and out the doors, she felt his hand leave her back. She shivered a little at the sudden cold on the spot he had touched. *Focus,* she demanded to herself.

Betty and her small family were forming a line so they would talk to neighbors and friends who had come to pay their respects. Evie hugged Clementine, squeezing her extra hard. The twelve-year-old had taken Bill's passing badly. He had been the only father she had ever had, since her own had dropped her off when she wasn't even out of diapers and had never returned. She was going to be a tall girl, like her tall, hunky cousin Jasper with black hair and brown eyes like him also.

Moving down, Evie hugged Grandma Betty, the only grandma she had ever had. Bill's death had made Evie realize that one day Betty would die too. The older woman had been a rock in Evie's world for so long she didn't know what she would ever do without the older woman.

Then she moved to Jasper—she had to hug him, it would look odd if she didn't. Taking a deep breath, she put her arms around him like she had done with the others. But this time, she felt something very different. She all but melted into his perfect body. Feeling protected by his large body, it felt so good to be there. He was over six feet tall and towered over her short five foot three inches.

"Sorry for your loss." She managed to push away when she knew she had hugged him for too long.

He squeezed her once more as he said, "You lost him too." When he let her go, she was crying again. Damn it, she hated funerals.

Heading out the door to the hot, sunny day that had just been added to the tally of worst days of her life, Evie waited. Wiping her eyes and waiting for her sisters to come out of the church, she rubbed her hands over her face. This one had been bad, and her emotions had been all over the place. What was wrong with her? Had it been so long since a man had actually touched her that when Jasper held her hand her, she went all crazy? She had never felt the electricity that had bounced between them in her life. And that included the year she had been married. But Greg had never made her feel half of what Jasper had with one touch of his hand.

Get it together, Evie, she said to herself as her sisters, Ben, and Gabe followed her into the sunshine.

"That was awful," Zoey said as soon as she made it out the church.

"No kidding," Della agreed. "That one part of the sermon had me in tears."

"I know. That was a perfect sermon for Bill, didn't you think so, Evie?" Zoey asked.

"Yeah, tears." Evie had heard none of it. She should have tried to pay more attention. "It was very good."

"Best part, coming in a close second was Jasper in that suit, wow." Zoey fanned her face with her hands.

"Hey." Her fiancé grabbed her around her waist and pulled her to him. "No looking at other men."

Zoey laughed and leaned back into the man she loved. "He's not a man, he's Jasper. You don't need to be jealous of Jasper in his sexy suit, love. He can never look better than you do."

"Thanks, I think," Gabe said and kissed her baby sister on the top of the head.

"I've seen you both naked, and he doesn't hold a candle to you." Zoey laughed again as he carried her to their car.

"See you at Betty's," Zoey called from his arms.

Della and Evie watched as their sister was carried off. Della said in amusement, "We will just put them on cleanup, since we won't be seeing them for a while."

"Good thinking," Evie said. "We better get going, since we should be at Betty's before everyone starts arriving." They were serving the food for the mourners who were bound to show up after the funeral.

"Little Jasper has grown up, hasn't he?" Della asked as they walked to Evie's pickup.

"I hadn't noticed," Evie lied.

"You are a widow, Evie, not dead. Maybe you should take a look." Della slid her sunglasses over her green eyes.

"He's younger than Zoey, Della," Evie reminded Della. Or maybe she was reminding herself. Zoey was four years Evie's junior. Making him five years younger than her.

"Age has nothing to do with it," Della said. "Eye candy is eye candy."

"How about we think of him as more than eye candy? He's a nice guy. He is more than a nice butt." Evie tried to turn the conversation. "Let's get going before the crowd beats us to Betty's."

Della smiled and grabbed Evie's arm as they walked. "You're right, we need to get going. But he does have a nice butt. I am glad you can still notice that in your advanced stage of widowhood."

Evie groaned, why had she even said that? Why couldn't she just let it go? Now she had to spend the next few hours trying not to look at him in his sexy suit and not look at his butt. And also, avoiding Della with her smart comments on the entire situation. It was going to be a long day.

CHAPTER 2

Jasper Reed was tired of making polite conversation with people who asked the same questions. Was he surprised that his grandpa had passed so suddenly in his sleep? Unexpected, wasn't it? What was going to happen to the farm now? Was Evie going to do the harvest this year?

The questions grated on his nerves. Of course, it was a complete shock when he got the call about his grandpa, because the man was never supposed to die. Who knows what would happen with the farm, it was up to Grandma Betty to decide. It was not his place to make that decision for her.

And everyone kept asking about Evie. It was starting to be a bit annoying. She was on everybody's mind. It didn't matter that she had been helping Grandpa Bill since she was a teenager, but now it seemed like she was going to take over. He had been telling everyone that he was going to be completing Grandpa Bill's last harvest. Not Evie, although he had not added that to anyone but himself. When he had gotten the news that Grandpa had died without finishing the harvest, Jasper had decided he needed to complete it for the man who had been his father.

Now he was going to finish what his grandpa had not been able to.

The harvest. He had taken the next week off from work to finish the wheat crop that was still in the fields. Then in a month or so he would take two weeks and return to do the corn. Once the harvests were over, Grandma Betty could decide what to do with the farm next.

Jasper looked around his grandma's yard and noticed that most of the neighbors were leaving. His grandma had gone inside the house hours ago, she needed to get away from the crowd. Clem and Ben were playing catch. Zoey and her boyfriend were picking up plastic plates and cups from the dozens of folding tables that were set up on the side lawn. They were talking quietly and laughing together.

Shoving his hands in his pockets he decided he needed to get away from here. Heading behind the house, he decided to try to find the trail that he and his grandpa had made the summer he was ten. It was still there. Clem must use it now. He couldn't believe the man was gone. Now what? At this point in his life he didn't want to farm, he liked his job as an accountant in downtown Minneapolis. He loved dealing in numbers, not corn and wheat seed. When he had been younger, he had always thought his future was on this piece of land, but the older he got the more he enjoyed making numbers tally to what he wanted them to add up to.

Making his way through the small woods, the path opened up to the field beyond it. Pale gold wheat as far as the eyes could see dancing in the wind. Grandpa's wheat. Stopping to watch its movements he noticed her standing in the field, looking at the sun setting in the distance. Evie Hart. She may go by her married name now, but should would always be a Hart to him. Standing waist deep in the tall wheat with her arms stretched out touching just the tips of the wheat stocks at her fingertips. His breath lodged in his throat. She was beautiful.

Her loose hair was trailing down her back and disappeared into the tall stocks. The hair was the exact color of the wheat she was standing in. Every time he saw a wheat field ready for harvest, he thought of Evie and her hair. Both of her sisters had bright red hair but Evie had golden yellow hair, which always made her stand out in the sister group. He had rarely seen her hair loose like today. It looked amazing. It was always braided and usually it was hanging down to her cute little butt. He had first noticed that butt in the middle of this very wheat field when he was fifteen, and she had been twenty and had bent down to pick up the hat the wind had blown off her head. He had just happened to notice how her shorts fit her perfectly. The sight of the woman's butt had made a big impression on a boy in the middle of puberty and Jasper had had a crush on the older woman ever since.

Evangelina Hart had been the measuring stick that every woman Jasper ever met was measured against. They had to be blond and bonus points for green eyes. They had to be fun and easy to talk to. He had yet to meet one that came close to perfection, just the original.

He should let her know he was here, but he hated to disturb her. Or did he hate not being able to stare at her? He had spent the afternoon catching little glimpses of her moving gracefully through the crowds of people. She knew everyone and had a word to say to all of them. She had made it look effortless.

He had been a little angry at his Grandma Betty when he had gotten to the funeral to find the Hart's included in the family. They were just neighbors. But as he sat between his grandma and Evie, he realized they were family for Betty. She had raised the sisters just like she had raised Jasper and now Clem. The sister's mother had taken off when they were young, and Betty had taken over the role of mother in their lives for years. And when their dad, Charley, had died five years ago, Bill had stepped into that role for them. Jasper had spent many holidays with the Hart sisters over the years.

"Evie," he called out and started into the field.

Evie spun toward him, her hair flying from her head in her haste. "Jasper."

"How are you doing?" He was close enough to see her eyes were bright with tears. The makeup she had on during the funeral was long gone.

"Good, I guess. Are people leaving yet?" she asked.

"Yes, finally. I am so tired of people," he admitted.

"I hate funerals. I have been to way too many," Evie said more to herself than to him.

"I know, I hate them too," Jasper agreed.

Neither spoke for a moment as the wind blew around them. Jasper watched as Evie picked a stock of wheat, placed it between her hands and rubbed them together. She opened her hands and blew the chaff from her hands and held up the wheat seed that remained. Jasper couldn't take his eyes off her, did she know how she affected him? She was beautiful in everything she did.

"The wheat is ready," Evie said, looking into his eyes that had been watching her hands. He hoped to god she didn't see that her movements turned him on.

"Do you want me ..." she said.

"Yes," he whispered.

She finished with, "to start harvest tomorrow?" Then she stopped and said, "What?"

Jasper ran his hands through his black hair as her words hit him right in the gut, or maybe lower. "Harvest, yes."

"Okay, that's the plan." She looked at his hair, he knew he had just messed it up, but he liked how she was staring at it. Then she added, "I better get home."

She brushed past him and he rubbed his hands over his face, he said, "No, no, no. I don't want you to start tomorrow."

"What?" She spun around to face him, questions in her green eyes.

"I am going to harvest Grandpa's last crop. By myself. I don't need you." Jasper hoped he sounded more confident about it than he felt.

"When? Don't you have to go back to work?" Evie said.

"I took some time off to finish with the wheat. I will do it myself," he said with more conviction.

"You can't," Evie stated firmly.

"I can." Now he was getting mad at her. She didn't think he could harvest a crop, but he knew she was wrong.

"Not alone," she insisted.

"Alone." Folding his arms in frustration. He didn't think the hardest part of all this would be convincing Evie he didn't need her help. Couldn't she understand he needed to do this for his grandfather?

"Quit being stubborn, Jasper, it would take you a week to get this off by yourself." She ran her hands lightly over the tops of the wheat stocks again.

"It will not," he insisted trying not to watch her eyes looking at the golden stocks all around them.

"Yes," she said and started listing things on her fingers. "First it takes at least an hour to get to town and back in that old truck with a load of grain, if there is no line. Second, it will take you another hour or so to fill the truck up again. Third, you only have about seven hours in the day that you can combine. Fourth, it is going to rain in three days so that will have you stopped in your tracks."

"Fifth?" he asked sarcastically.

He watched her face knowing she had nothing for five, but her mind was digging to find something. He watched her face light up and she held up her hand with all fingers up and said in triumph, "Fifth, if nothing breaks. I know you can't fix anything that breaks. I, and only I, can fix it."

She was even cute when she was being smug. He thought she might do a victory dance, and he wanted to see it. But no dance came. "I can find someone else to fix it."

"Bull, nobody works on our stuff but me." Liking how she said "our stuff" he almost laughed at her antics.

She had the gift of being able to fix anything big or small on the farm. His grandfather had nicknamed her MacGyver years ago, whenever anything broke Grandpa Bill would always say, "Let's have MacGyver look at it." And that woman would always get it going again. Rarely was she stumped when it came to machines or equipment.

Watching as she changed the five fingers to one and blew on it at him. She said, "See you in the morning. It should only take two days."

Turning she walked out of the field and down the tree path toward the Reed house. Planted to the ground staring after her in that moment all the anger and frustration were gone, he had never wanted a woman more than he wanted Evie at that moment. The blue dress was form fitting and about three inches too short, and it made Jasper's body ache to touch her again.

He hadn't really meant to touch her during the funeral, but when she had grabbed his hand, he had been unable to let go of it. He had spent more time than he had wanted to admit looking at the little hand on his leg. It was then that he noticed that she was still wearing her wedding ring even after over a decade as a widow. The gold band was beautiful on her hand, but it shouldn't have been there. To Jasper, it was just a reminder of the man she had been married to, a man not worth remembering.

By chance their hands had moved and his hand had pressed against her leg. Almost touching the bare skin of her leg, her skirt was so short and even shorter when she sat. He'd moved his leg to trap their hands so he wouldn't start caressing her leg with the back if his hand.

Then after the service he had touched her back, again without planning it. He'd been shocked when he noticed through her hair that she had a small tattoo of a heart on her back. He had to touch it to make sure it was real. Evie had never struck him as the tattoo type. But there she had one—a heart right on her spine between her shoulder blades. The size of a quarter and only the outline of a red heart. He couldn't not touch it, not touch her.

How was he going to handle two days working beside her? During an hour long funeral service for his own grandfather, he

had found dozens of excuses to touch the woman. Two days was going to be impossible.

CHAPTER 3

THE NEXT DAY, the morning routine at the Singleton house began the same as it did every day. Evie got up, showered, and got dressed for the day, then she woke her son so he could get ready as she made breakfast. They would eat together until the bus came and picked up her growing boy. Before Evie could get the plates cleared from the table, her sister Zoey would show up and they would start their work.

Today was going to start like most mornings with weeding in the gardens that grew their vegetables for the farmer's markets, their main source of income. That and a few hundred acres of corn this year. All before they could start combining for the day.

Evie loved the gardens and only grew the corn and wheat on an altering rotation because she had yet to make enough to get by from just the farmer's market. The wheat years were much easier than the corn, because the corn was claustrophobic once it grew over two feet tall. But there was money in the stuff, so she grew it. The other reason was that she loved how the wheat waved in the wind. She loved watching the movement of the stocks—it was like the ocean. When she had seen the ocean for the first time, a few years ago on a vacation with Zoey and Della, she fell in love with the constant movement. So much like wheat.

It had been almost six months since Zoey moved home and it had been an interesting adventure. The sisters got along and farmed together well since both were early risers, Evie due to her years of farming with their dad, and Zoey because of her time in the Army. By starting their days early, the two were able to end early when possible to spend time with their families in the late afternoon. At the same time to the point that they didn't even need to discuss what thing should be done next.

When she was only eighteen, Zoey had been forced to make the decision to go to jail or join the Army when she had been accused of starting a fire in the high school. She had been out of control and the chief of police and their dad, Charley, had decided that she needed discipline and the military was the way to get it. After eight years, she had come back to the farm, but had returned nearly broken from her time in Afghanistan. The only stories Zoey ever told about her time in Afghanistan had been fun and happy ones, but Evie knew there were other stories she never told to anyone. Well maybe Gabe, but not her sisters.

It had taken weeks for Zoey to begin acting like the Zoey who left. And it had taken months to get back to the real outgoing and fun loving Zoey. Evie liked to think she had helped the most, but she knew Gabe had been the real one behind the change.

Evie had a hard time with her baby sister's man at first and still was a little suspicious of him. But she had seen enough to know he was exactly what her sister needed. The age gap between them— almost thirteen years—had bothered Evie, but they were in love, very much so. They loved to be together and loved to touch and kiss for no reason all the time. It drove Evie up a tree, because they were adults and should be able to control that.

Maybe it bothered her because that was not the relationship she had ever had with her husband. Seeing them made her want a love like that for herself. Evie knew her cute little redheaded sister deserved the love and attention of her man, but she also knew that there was not a man out there who would treat her or love her like that. Those types are few and far between.

Just before the dew had gone out of the grass Evie headed over to the Reeds to get the combine ready for the day. She headed over and walked into the giant shed beyond the house, really hoping she wouldn't run into Jasper until Zoey showed up. They could pal around like the old days and ignore her, she was just fine with that.

Her luck was running high when she found the shed was empty. Grabbing a wrench she opened a side panel and started working on the huge combine in the quiet.

"Is this sabotage or actual work?" Jasper's voice caused her to jump, hitting the heavy panel above her head.

"Actual work," she said as the heavy panel slammed onto her head, stopping her words. Her head must have dislodged the latch that kept it open.

"Evie." She heard him exclaim from the other side of the panel, before it lifted slowly from her head.

"I guess the combine was not impressed with what I was doing." She came out and moved away from the offending machine, rubbing her head with both hands, still holding the wrench. "That might leave a mark."

She felt him take the wrench from her hand and watched as he dropped it on the ground. His hands replaced hers on her head, gently running his fingers through her hair, and massaging her scalp. "I don't see any bleeding. Are you dizzy?"

His gentle massage was making her dizzy, but not from the bang on the head. "No." Why was she breathless?

She felt his hands leave her hair, but they just moved to the side of her head and lifted her face to look into his eyes. *Brown pools of milk chocolate*, she thought. Did she really get knocked out and this was a dream? Was he going to kiss her? She hoped he was going to kiss her. But instead he just held her gaze.

"Your eyes are fine," he said.

"Yours are too," she responded. Probably not how he meant it.

"Does your head hurt?" His mouth lifted at the corners slightly, but still held her gaze.

"I hit it on the combine," she said, as if he hadn't been there.

"I know." Then he ran his fingers through her hair again.

She put her hands on her head and hair after his left. "You messed up my hair."

"I was checking for bleeding and for bumps," he explained, dropping his hands and shoving them into his pockets. Jeans today and a soft blue T-shirt.

"But you messed up my hair. It's all pulled out." She tried to push and pull it back into place so she didn't have to take the time to braid it again.

"I thought you were bleeding, woman!" Jasper said with sudden anger. "I thought you were going to pass out."

"I wasn't going to pass out." Trying to ignore that he was watching her mess with her hair, Evie knew she would have to redo her hair since she could feel that it was completely messed up. It would look even worse later if she left it alone. Pulling out the ponytail elastic at the end of her braid she put it in her mouth. With her teeth clamped around the elastic she said, "I was barely hit. It sounded worse than it was."

"I didn't know that." His hands were still in his pockets, but she knew he was watching as she unbraided her hair. She glanced at his eyes, staring at her hair.

When she got the last bit undone, she said to him still clinching the elastic between her teeth, "Did you want to check one more time so when I get this back together you won't wreck it again?"

"No, no, I'm good." His voice actually sounded deeper than before, probably just her imagination.

Running her fingers through her hair she didn't feel anything but a small bump on the side of her head. Once she got the locks straight, she started braiding it again. Looking up at him she noticed he was still staring at her hair and his dark brown eyes were glittering like they had yesterday in the wheat field. Dark chocolate pools that Evie wanted to jump right into. She held that dark gaze until she took the elastic from her teeth and wrapped it around the end of the braid. She dropped the braid over her shoulder and it landed right over her breast. His eyes followed, landing on her breasts under her red flannel work shirt.

It was at that point that Zoey walked into the shed, talking as she went. "Are we ready to get this thing started?"

Both Evie and Jasper jumped at the interruption. Neither answered the bubbly redhead, but both looked away from each other.

"What is going on?" Zoey asked.

"The combine tried to eat Evie," Jasper joked, but his voice was huskier than usual and his hands were still stuffed into his pockets.

"Jasper came in and scared me. Then the door closed on my head," Evie explained, wondering what would have happened if Zoey hadn't showed up right then.

Zoey turned to her sister in concern. "Are you okay?"

"Don't touch the hair, she has a thing about the hair," Jasper said.

Evie shot him a look over her sister's shoulder. "He messed it up. I had to redo the braid. I hate rebraiding it."

"Maybe you should cut it, it wouldn't be an issue if it was shorter." Zoey had been saying that for a while now, she herself had a short hairdo that she insisted was easier to take care of, but Evie wasn't ready yet. Maybe she would never be ready.

"If she likes it, leave her alone, little Zoey," Jasper said.

Pivoting on Jasper, Zoey pushed him in the chest, "Don't call me little Zoey." Everyone used to call her that nickname due to her short stature. Barely five feet tall, she had been mercilessly picked on for it when she was younger. Oddly Evie at five foot three was the tallest of the three sisters. They were a short little group.

"Okay, I won't," he regained his balance. Then changed the topic. "What is the plan?"

Evie's mind had abandoned her. What *were* they planning? Her mind pushed away the look on Jasper's face as he looked at her breasts and the plan popped back in. She explained to the other two, "Start west and work our way back to the barn. Jasper can combine and Zoey and I can take turns working over at the farm on everything that needs to be done there."

"Sounds good," the other two said together.

"Unless either of you have a different plan." Evie had been working to temper her 'take charge' personality since Zoey called her out on it a few months ago. She was still overly conscious about being too bossy.

But it didn't help that sometimes Zoey expected her to be in charge. Knowing when to be or not be bossy was sometimes a challenge.

"No, I think it's a good one," Zoey said. "Jasper?"

"Sounds good."

With the plan in place, the three set out to start Bill's last harvest. *Bill's last harvest.* Evie fought back the tears as she followed the other two out of the shed.

CHAPTER 4

JASPER HAD FORGOTTEN in the last few years how much he loved driving the combine. It was big and cumbersome but it made you feel very powerful sitting ten feet in the air with the big motors running below you. Jasper had not driven the combine since the summer he had graduated from college. Unable to find a job for months he had spent the summer at the farm. He remembered Evie hadn't been around much to help that year, but maybe that was because Grandpa Bill had him and didn't need any more help than that.

Evie had refreshed his memory of driving the combine before they left the yard, but he had remembered most of it when he climbed into the roomy cab. With him in the driver's seat she had climbed into the cab and started pointing out what levers and knobs did. It was especially difficult to concentrate on her explanations with her nearly on his lap. How he had managed to not pull her onto his lap and tell her he knew how to drive the damn machine, he didn't know.

He had just let her talk until she was satisfied he was ready before she left the machine, slamming the door closed behind her. She climbed down the combine's steps and vanished for what felt like forever and Jasper was about to get up to make sure she was okay when she stepped into view. Waving to indicate she was clear of the machine, and he was ready to go.

Starting a long day in the field with the Hart sisters. He was still thinking he could have done it without them, but it was going to be more fun with Evie around.

***

Hours later he was missing his grandpa and regretting not coming back to help his grandpa more often. After so many years away he was surprised he was enjoying himself as much as he was. Much of the work was like second nature to him still. But he was always looking for the old man to show up.

Now he was watching the grain truck turn off the gravel road into the field, and he wondered who was driving this time. After he spent the day analyzing and guessing which sister would emerge from the cab, he thought he finally had it figured out. Evie drove slower and could maneuver into position with ease, but Zoey drove too fast and usually took two or more tries to get in position. Both were fun to watch, but he found himself looking forward to Evie's arrivals more. Zoey rarely left the cab, but Evie always left the truck and walked around the combine checking things out.

On her second trip Jasper had jumped out and joined her, to see what she was up to. She'd looked a little annoyed at him following her, but he couldn't talk to her about it since the combine was too loud to actually have a conversation on the ground around it. At first he wanted to see what she was doing, but the end he just wanted to see her.

With a smile, he realized it was Evie with the cautious driving and exacting parking. This time he decided not to mess with her, he just let her do her thing. But to his surprise, she climbed up the ladder to the cab. Having shed her flannel shirt hours ago, she was wearing just a tank top. It was near ninety degrees so Jasper didn't expect her to wear the thick shirt all day, but Evie in a tank top was hard to ignore. It was loose and green to match her eyes but did nothing to hide the curve of her breasts.

She opened the door to the cab, then turned to shut it behind her. His breath caught at the flash of her tattoo in plain view. He hadn't noticed it earlier in the day, but there it was. So not something Evie would do, but there it was.

Turning around she said, "You take the truck this time, stop at your grandma's, and eat. Zoey will meet you there and take the grain truck to town. The next load will be the last of the day."

Jasper looked at his watch, it was after suppertime. The day had flown by. "What about your son? Don't you need to feed him?"

She frowned. "Your grandma is watching him for me."

"Does she do that a lot?" he asked and had no idea why. His grandma had always watched Ben when Evie needed her to, and Grandma had loved having him around.

"About as much as I watch Clem, I guess we don't keep track of time." The frown grew a little deeper, and she was starting to sound mad.

"Never mind." He wanted to let it go, he didn't even know why he had brought it up. It didn't matter if she spent time with her son or not.

"No, do you think I am taking advantage of your grandma?" Her chin shot out at the question.

"No, I am just saying you have a family you should go home to. I can finish this," he said and stood up.

"My son understands that I am helping a neighbor out, he likes to spend time with your family." She had to look up to meet his gaze. The cab had just become very small with them both standing in the small space.

"Fine." He didn't move, just looked down at her. Having riled her up, he had no idea what to do with it. Her nose flared as she breathed. Over the years he had seen her temper flare, but he had rarely caused it. This was the first time it was directed right at him.

"Do what you want then." She turned and grabbed the door handle.

What had he tried to achieve by pissing her off? Had he wanted to see her mad, see if he could get a reaction out of her?

Before she could get the door open he said, "I'm sorry. I said that wrong. You have a family you could and should be spending time with, I can finish this. Go spend time with your son."

She turned to him and said, "I know I have a son. I spend as much time with him as I can every day. But every once in a while, my priority is somewhere else. Like getting this wheat off the field before it rains. He is almost eleven and understands that. I ate supper with him and Clem and Grandma Betty, now it is your turn to go eat. I will work out here." Her anger was still there but better under control.

"I was wrong," he admitted knowing she was right. From everything he knew about her she was a great mom and her son was lucky to have her. He couldn't even explain why he was trying to pick a fight with her. But he knew he was.

He stepped back as far as the small space allowed to let her by, but before she could move the machine made a loud banging sound. Diving past him she knocked him off balance, and he grabbed at the close walls to keep upright. Most of her body made it past him and she grabbed a lever and pushed it up. Whatever she had done stopped the spinning parts, leaving the cab eerily quiet.

She was half lying across him and half in the seat. "This is why you need me," she said pointing at him as she righted herself in the seat.

Getting up she grabbed him by the arms and spun him in an odd dance before pushing him into the seat. She was practically laughing when she turned and reached above her head for something near the ceiling. Watching her stretch to reach the high ceiling, he almost groaned when her tank top pulled free of her pants and showed an inch of skin. His hands itched to touch the pale skin that was exposed.

Finding the wrench she was looking for she turned with a smile and showed him her prize. But Jasper did not even notice whatever she was so proud of, all he could see was how her tank top had bunched up, highlighting every contour of her breast. He could not tear his eyes away. Without noticing his stare, she tugged her shirt down and turned to open the door, hurrying down the steps.

Jasper stayed in the cab for a while, trying to get his body under control. By the time he made it out of the cab he realized he had wasted that time, because when he finally reached her, she was standing on her tiptoes trying to reach a bolt above her head with a wrench. She was a few inches too short and once again her shirt had pulled high and the toned stomach above her jeans was showing.

Walking up behind her, he grabbed her around the waist—right where that bare patch was—and lifted her the few inches she needed.

"Thanks." He heard her say. Holding her as she worked, his hands slid higher up to her rib cage as she wiggled. He was trying to keep his hands from slipping, but she wiggled again and then gave one hard jerk of her arm. She slipped from his grasp and she slid down to the ground. When she finally landed on her feet on the hard ground, each of his hands were holding a perfect bare breast.

"Done," she was rigid in his arms and as breathless as he was.

His mind was telling him to let go of her breasts, but his hands had a mind of their own and would not listen. She had fallen back against his body and he held her there in an intimate hold. How many times had he dreamed of doing just this over the years? Too many to count.

"I'm on the ground now," she whispered. If he wasn't holding her so close, he would not have heard her.

He forced his hands to let go of her breasts, but with a mind of their own they slid down the path they had slipped up, running across her flat stomach, and ending on the skin at her waist just where her pants started. It was only then that he was able to let her go and take a step back. If she hadn't noticed his erection yet, he had no way of hiding it now and really didn't want to hide it anymore. What he wanted was her breasts back in his hands.

"I think I got it fixed, it sometimes gets loose and has to be tightened. Thanks for the lift, sorry I fell on you in the end." Fumbling as she tugged her shirt down and bent to pick up the wrench that must have fallen when she did. Her words sounded like nothing had actually happened, but her hands were shaking with the wrench in her hand.

Stepping close to her again, he looked into her green eyes as she met his gaze. Smiling down at her, he said, "The end was the best part."

Turning away from her, he walked away. All he really wanted to do was touch her again. Pull her into his arms. Now he knew her breasts fit in his hands perfectly, and he wanted them back.

Leaving her with the combine, he drove the truck to his grand-mother's house for supper. Just as Evie had promised, Zoey was there to take the load of grain to town so he could eat.

Both kids were there and though they had already eaten with Evie, they both joined him for dessert while Jasper ate the meatloaf his grandma had made. Evie's son turned out to be a fun kid who was smart, loved to tell jokes, and always listened to Grandma Betty. Tonight, he also found himself looking at the boy and finding his mother in almost every feature. The most prominent was the blond hair and green eyes. The only features Jasper knew that hadn't come from Evie were the dimples in his cheeks and his height; Ben was going to be tall.

While he ate, he listened to the two middle schoolers talk about life. School had started the week before and both seemed to be liking it. He knew Clem loved school and excelled and assumed Ben did too. They reminded him of him and Zoey at that age. Those were fun years, before Zoey started to think he was lame and started to run with a wilder group. He hoped these two didn't end up drifting apart as they grew older.

When Zoey returned, he took over the truck, and she went home for the day. Parking in the proper spot back at the end of the field he waited, no way was he getting out after he had felt her up. *Just wait for the truck to be full and leave. Just ignore the combine driver.* And he would have managed to avoid her if she hadn't climbed into the truck through the passenger door.

"I think we are almost done for the night." She was still wearing shorts and a tank top. But she obviously had gotten chilly in the evening air since her nipples were visible under her tank top. She was not wearing a bra today, as Jasper was well aware of.

"Okay," was all he could manage.

"You can take this load to town and then come back for another. But that one, just leave it in the shed and we can take it in to town tomorrow morning," she explained, as she slipped on a flannel shirt that had been laying on the truck's seat. But the image was still there, playing on repeat in his mind. "Or do you want to drive the combine?"

"No, you can."

He did not want to move because he was not in charge of his body. Ever since he saw her nipples and had remembered how they felt in his hand. He needed her out of the truck. Dragging her over to his side of the cab was starting to sound like a great idea. She had no idea how good she looked. She never had.

"Okay, I'll meet you in the yard when you get back from town." With that, she jumped out of the cab and slammed the door. Watching her walk away he wished he had the nerve to act on his feelings, just once.

Later when Jasper got back from town, Evie was in the yard waiting. Both kids were helping and she let them work the controls this time. When the truck was full, they moved everything into the shed for the night.

As he watched Evie and Ben walk home, he tried to decide if he had succeeded in keeping his hands to himself. Except for the double full-handed breast hold, he did good. Would he do better tomorrow or worse? Most of him was hoping for better, but there was a small part of him that was cheering for worse. That was probably the part that had actually held her breasts.

CHAPTER 5

EVIE WAS DREADING the day in front of her. She had already fed and watered all the animals at Zoey and Gabe's place. The sisters raised chickens and pigs for meat that they sold at the farmer's markets. It was Saturday and Zoey and Gabe had already headed out before dawn to get to Minneapolis for the farmer's market. Usually it was Zoey and Evie but Evie had stayed behind to help Jasper finish with the wheat. Once Ben got up he would head over to Betty's and spend the day there with Clem.

Alone. She was going to be with him alone *all* day. No switching places with Zoey when she got too nervous around him. By the end of the day yesterday her nerves had been frayed. Every time she brought the truck out, he would follow her around when she was inspecting the equipment. What had he been doing? When she had stopped, he stopped and looked at the exact thing she was looking at. The machines had been too loud to have a conversation but his closeness was enough to make her nervous.

Then when they finally had a conversation, he just picked a fight with her about her parenting skills. He had barely been around in seven years, so he had no idea what kind of parent she was. It still made her bristle just thinking about it.

After he had gotten her all riled up, *it* had happened. Evie didn't even know what to call the encounter. One minute she was trying to get the nut tight that always came loose, the next he was lifting her up so she could reach it. It had felt so good to have his hands on her; his warm hands on her bare skin had messed with her mind. Then she had gotten it tightened just as he lost his grip on her waist and she had felt those warm hands slide up her body. When she came to a stop, he was cupping her bare breasts in his warm hands. Every voice in her head begged his hands to move, to caress, and not to leave her breasts. Sanity had returned, and he had moved his hands but had caressed her body as he did so.

She had walked away too embarrassed to look at him. What must he think of her acting like that? Had he realized how much she had enjoyed the contact? She hoped not. She had just let Jasper touch her breasts and not just a small touch. Jasper was just a kid. She should have known better. He may have turned into a handsome, drool-worthy man, but he was still a kid to her. A kid who made her insides quiver when he held her breasts.

Time to get this over with, she decided as she walked up Betty's driveway. Hopefully she could control her wanton ways today, she at least hoped she could.

When she made it to the house Betty and Jasper were both waiting for her on the front step and Evie was unable to say anything. Jasper was his sexy self in a plain green T-shirt and cargo shorts. Betty broke the awkward moment between by saying, "No Zoey today?"

Evie got it together. "No, she and Gabe are at the Minneapolis Farmer's Market today. We can't miss out on it even if it is harvest. So, it's just me today."

Betty laughed and said, "You are enough, Evie. Right, Jasper? All you need is Evie."

Evie didn't think Jasper was going to answer until she heard him agree, "Yes, all I need is Evie."

Then he stepped off the porch and Evie suddenly though he was going to take her into his arms, but he turned at the last moment and started walking toward the shed.

Smiling at Betty she said, "We should finish today, Ben will be over when he gets up. I better get going."

Then she walked after Jasper and wondered what she would have done had he actually pulled her into his arms. Would she have just let it happen and see how it turned out? Or would she do the right thing and push him away? Most likely that one, probably.

Jasper was already in the shed getting the combine out, so she headed for the truck that he had left in the yard after bringing last night's load into town earlier today. Watching him maneuver the giant machine out of the yard, she followed him slowly out to the field. It was going to be a long day.

They easily fell into the same rhythm they had set the previous day. He didn't even follow her around when she was inspecting the combine. It was actually over two hours after starting that she actually spoke to Jasper, and that was to switch places with him so he could have lunch with his grandmother. After he had returned from lunch, he kept driving the truck and she had stayed in the combine.

Trying not to take his attitude personally she couldn't help but feel he was in a bad mood because what had happened yesterday. As the hours progressed, she spent more time dwelling on it. Should she apologize? What would she say? Sorry you touched my boobs? She had no idea.

A short reprieve came when in late afternoon the kids came out with Jasper and they each took a turn riding in the combine and the truck. Ben enjoyed spending time out in the fields but Clem loved it even more. Having been convinced for years that Clem would take over Bill's farm when the time came, Evie was sad Bill's death had occurred while Clem was only thirteen. She hoped that Betty would just rent out the land for a while, so Clem could take it over in a decade.

When suppertime came around, the kids decided to run back to Betty's instead of riding in the truck with Jasper. Evie watched them race through the stubble across the field, she loved that they were such good friends. Maybe one day that would change, but Evie would enjoy it while it lasted.

Jasper was still moody when he brought her a sandwich an hour or so after the kids left. He volunteered to keep making the trips into town with the grain truck. For Evie, this day could not end soon enough. Her eyes wouldn't stop following Jasper when he was near, oddly missing him when he was not. All she needed was to get away from him for a few hours and get her head on straight.

The sky was turning pink with the sunset as she watched him drive the truck across the field from her position on the top step of the combine. This last trip had taken him longer than any other all day so she had parked and shut off the combine as she waited. Stepping outside she had not realized how muggy it was outside still until she had sat down. The sun still had about an hour before it set as Jasper parked the truck in the steamy evening and walked over to her. He was still in those shorts but his shirt was gone, it had vanished sometime after lunch. The old truck had no air conditioning and it got hot in the cab he had been riding around in all day.

"Something break?" he asked.

"No, you're just late," she said.

"Sorry, everyone is trying to beat the rain."

"That's okay. I was enjoying the sauna." She smiled, hoping his mood would improve as the day was ending.

"Yeah it's hot out tonight. Do you think we will get rain?" he asked.

"Yes, it will rain by morning." She climbed down the steps. It was even hotter on the ground.

"I think so, too." He was looking over at the sunset in the west.

"You go ahead and finish harvesting the last of the wheat in this field. Once you're done come back to the yard, what's left won't fill the combine. I'll take the truck to the shed and we can deal with this little bit after the rain stops," she said, knowing that it would be her and Zoey who would deal with the grain after the rain. Jasper would be back at work.

"Okay," he said. He climbed up into the cab of the combine and the machine roared to life.

Once the truck was full of the wheat she had already collected and Jasper had left, she pulled the tarp over the full truck bed. If she was going to leave the grain in the truck for a while, she liked to have it covered even if it was a hassle. What was in the combine would have to stay in there until the rain was over.

After getting all the straps tightened, she saw the combine turn back toward her for its next pass. Evie shook her head., This thing with Jasper and her wasn't going to make her miss finishing the harvest. She walked over to the combine and Jasper stopped the machine so she could climbed the steps. "Can I ride one last round? Bill's last wheat harvest."

When she and Bill had planted the field, she could never imagine that he wouldn't be here for the harvest. That Jasper would be the one in the combine and not Bill himself. That next time it wouldn't be either Bill or Jasper in the combine. So much change.

"Yes." He smiled as she shut the door behind her.

"Thank you." She had hoped he would not kick her out. But she would understand if he had, it had been a trying two days.

"You have more of a right to be here than me," he said as the machine started forward. She squatted down and held on with one hand on the seat and the other braced against the wall.

She couldn't stop herself from saying, "You wore shorts today."

"You did too." He looked down at her.

"It's just odd that you wore shorts for combining, most men wear jeans." She had been thinking about those shorts all day.

"Too hot for jeans. And most women wear shoes to combine." He pointedly looked at her feet and the big plastic sandals on them.

"They're sandals." She liked being able to kick them off whenever she wanted to in the big machine.

"You don't wear them when you combine. It's just your little feet running this big machine," he said.

When had he noticed she didn't wear shoes in the combine? Was he paying attention to her? It felt strange to think someone noticed what she did.

Watching the standing grain as it was cut and slowly disappeared beneath the combine was a mesmerizing sight. She could watch the repetitive motion all day—had on occasion. Whispering more to herself than to him, she said, "Couldn't you just watch that all day? Wheat is beautiful."

Gazing up at him she saw he was looking at her. "Yes, it is." He ran a hand over her hair.

Gasping at the look in his eyes, she realized he had shut down some engines of the combine as the cab suddenly grew quiet. Distantly she registered that she could no longer feel the combine moving but she couldn't tear her eyes from his to see if it had. He was getting closer to her, that was the only movement she noticed.

His lips touched hers as his hand held her head in place—not that she would have been able to move as her body was frozen. Her only focus was on his mouth touching hers, once, twice, and the third time he gently bit her lower lip. She gasped at the fission that shot through her body. He took advantage of her open mouth and she felt his tongue touch hers. Hearing her moan at the touch, he deepened the kiss as his hand dug into her hair, pulling her head closer to his.

Her mind gained a small bit of control and she started to stand to stop this craziness. But as she got her feet under her, she felt herself being pulled onto his lap. But not just sitting on his lap, she was straddling him, and she was loving it. Just giving into those heady kisses that hadn't stopped. Letting herself just enjoy it while it lasted. Because she knew it wouldn't last long.

Feeling his hands in her hair, she was too distracted and before she knew what was happening, her hair was everywhere. He had unbraided it without her even realizing it.

He pulled back from the kiss, but he started nuzzling her neck and said, "Your hair is the color of August wheat and it's beautiful."

Evie moan at his words coupled with the fact that his hands were on her breasts. Today they were doing things that she had only dreamed they had done yesterday. Leaning her head back to give him better access she heard him groan as he started to kiss her on the exposed skin of her neck. She whimpered when his hands left her breasts under her tank top. She ran her hands up his chest over the muscles she had been wanting to touch for days.

"Evie, Evie, Evie," he said as his hand grabbed the shoulder straps of her tank top and pulled them down, exposing her breasts to his eyes and falling silent at the sight. His hands had dragged her shirt to her waist before lifting her body until she was kneeling. His hands moved to grasp her butt as his lips touched her breast.

"Jas," she said as she gasped. The sensation was almost more than she could take. She looked down as he began to suckle one of her breasts and unable to help herself, she grabbed his head to keep him from stopping. Never wanted the sensations running through her body to stop. She never wanted *him* to stop.

He pulled his head back a little and just looked at her, smiling a little before he said, "Evangelina Hart." Then he turned to her other breast.

Evie let her head fall back again as she let the sensation of his mouth on her breast wash over her. Both hands were anchored to his strong shoulders as his roamed her body with light touches. Running his hands up her inner thighs, sliding up under her shorts. She closed her eyes against the incredible sensations that were coursing through her body.

Her eyes flew open, and she gasped, "Jas," when she felt his finger run over her core. She hadn't thought it was possible to feel this good, and he had just increased the pleasure tenfold. Then he started to move that finger lightly over her core over and over and over again. Her hips started to move with the motion of his hand. Her head fell back again, and she moaned his name until she couldn't do anything but feel the orgasm roll through her body.

As her body recovered, she was putty in his hands, so he was able to touch and kiss her everywhere. She buried her head in his shoulder and tried to catch her breath and get the situation under control. But his hands were now running up and down her spine before stopping on her butt. She sat up and realized somehow he had gotten her clothes off. Naked on his lap, she grabbed her breasts to hide them from his gaze. As if he hadn't just kissed every inch of them and taken her over the edge with just his hands.

He grabbed her hands and put them on his chest and covered them with his own.. "I want to see them, I love your breasts, Evie Hart." Then he kissed her on the lips again, deepening it right away as his thumbs brushed against her sensitive nipples and she gasped.

One hand was gently kneading her breast as the other slid down across her stomach, which contracted at his touch. Then he moved lower to her core, and she groaned at the intimate touch. He brought her to the edge again with his hand, but just as she was about to go over she felt his penis replace his hand as he pushed into her.

She gasped, "Jas…per," as he entered her completely.

"I love when you say my name," he whispered as he sat holding her still, just getting used to him being inside her.

She couldn't say anything, because she couldn't breathe. Just feeling the sensation of him inside her, feeling so good. Then he pulled her up a little and gasped at the sensation flooding her body. She moved to see if it would happen again, and the delicious pulse washed over her once more. Wrapping his arms around her, Jasper matched her movements and Evie was lost to sensation. She could quickly feel herself losing control with Jasper and she was loving every second of it.'.

Feelings washed over her as with a flick of his finger to her core another orgasm took her over the edge. Evie felt Jasper follow her as his own orgasm rocked his body.

Her head was buried in his shoulder as his hand ran up and down her back, over her hair. Evie couldn't move if she wanted to, her limbs would not listen. Knowing that she needed to get out of the combine, because what just happened shouldn't have. But also needing to spend as much time in his arms as possible. Knowing she would never get to do this again so she had better enjoy it while it lasted.

Taking a deep breath, she started to say something but found she couldn't and just buried her head a little deeper. What to say after the best sex of your life?

"Don't be embarrassed, Evie," Jasper said.

"I am not." Pushing away from him she kept her eyes from meeting his.

"Then why won't you look at me?" he said.

"Okay, I am embarrassed. I am embarrassed that I took advantage of you." She climbed off his lap and grabbed her clothes from the floor.

"You did not take advantage of me," he argued.

"Of course I did. I took advantage of a kid," she bit out and turned to leave.

Before she could get the door handle to open, he grabbed her and spun her around. "I am not a kid. I think I just proved that to you."

Looking away from the anger in his eyes, she had never felt so vulnerable in her life as she stood naked holding her clothes to her chest. Staring into the angry eyes of a man who had shown her how good making love could be. A man who had in the last few days stolen a bit of her heart.

Don't cry in front of him, she demanded of herself as she shook. *Just get out of there.* Turning away from his angry eyes, she took a shaky breath. This time she was able to get the door open and walked out. She slammed the door behind her and realized she had to face him once more to walk down the ladder. When she turned, he was standing where she had left him in the cab with anger rolling off him. Her lip quivered as he disappeared out of sight as she climbed down.

Once she had gotten her feet on solid ground, she realized she had lost her shoes and knew she could not go back for them. As the tears started to fall into the now dark night, she started for the truck, knowing it would be a painful walk with no shoes even though it wasn't very far away. Hearing the combine start back up she knew he was finishing the field, not following her. Not that she wanted him to. Did she?

Pulling on her clothes as she walked, she forced herself not to look behind her. By the time she got to the truck she was fully clothed again. Happy with herself because she hadn't even looked behind her once. Except when she made sure he was moving again, but she had to make sure there were no issues. And maybe when that bird flew by, but who wouldn't.

Jumping into the truck, she drove faster than she usually did in the field to get out of there, not wanting to look again, because maybe she wanted him to follow her.

Parking in the Reed's shed she walked home. Jasper would have to deal with putting the combine away himself. There was no way she could face him again tonight.

She walked into the house and was glad Ben had come home and went to bed like he was supposed to. In the master bedroom, she walked right into the connected bathroom and shed the clothes she had so recently put on. Climbing into the shower, she let the hot water roll over her as her tears mixed with the water before swirling down the drain.

What had she done? Why had she touched him? She knew better. But more concerning was why did she crave his touch *again*? Why had it been Jasper who had touched her as no man had ever touched her? Why was it Jasper who given her an orgasm for the first time, and second? Why Jasper?

Shutting off the water she dried off and combed her hair before climbing into bed. She hoped that she would be able to sleep. As she drifted off, she knew she wouldn't just sleep—she would dream of Jasper's touch.

CHAPTER 6

IT HAD BEEN six weeks since Jasper had left his grandmother's house in the rain. Grandma Betty had insisted that the Harts would be able to take care of the grain in the truck and combine after he left. He didn't need to see that look in Evie's eyes again. As if what had happened in that combine had not been the best sex of his life. She had acted like he had been a kid who had no idea what they had done and it had pissed him off.

He should have followed her and told her he had wanted her since he first learned about sex. Should he have told her being with her was more than he had ever even dreamed of? That he was probably in love with the woman. But instead he had watched her walk away and had let her go.

For the last six weeks he had meant to leave the rest of the harvest to Evie. She didn't need him anyway. Deciding to leave her alone, get on with his life, and forget Evie Hart. He was thinking of asking out the first brunette he saw, except he didn't have the heart for dating yet.

What had happened in the combine had just been sex. It shouldn't have affected him this much. But it was sex with Evie and that made it so much more.

But yesterday Grandma Betty had called and said Evie had started on the corn crop, and he was in his car driving to Birch Cove by six o'clock the next morning. Hating that it was all that it took to get him back there.

Jasper had spent the six weeks realizing his work had suddenly lost its appeal. The numbers just ran together and he couldn't concentrate. He spent more time looking out his office window than he should have wishing that there was more open space in downtown Minneapolis. Each week he looked forward to the weekend so he could go to the farmer's market and see her. When Saturday finally arrived, he would force himself to stay away.

Now he was back at the farm, and he could barely see the combine churning through corn stocks at Zoey's house. He had thrown his stuff in his bedroom and headed out to find Zoey and her sister who had haunted his dreams.

It had been years since he had walked through the fields of the Hart family farm. This is where Evie, Zoey, and Della had been raised, in a house just down the road across from his grandparents. The last time he had been there, the house was empty. It had been since Charley had died when Jasper had been twenty. He had come home from college for the funeral, and it hadn't been easy to watch the sisters deal with Charley's passing.

Now the house looked lived in and even happier than it had in his memory. Charley had never been one for decorating or keeping the yard nice, but the fresh yellow paint on the house and flowers blooming by the front step made Jasper smile. Zoey was definitely making the house a home.

Since he had driven through Birch Cove he had been seen signs for 'Zoey's Pumpkin Patch' and here in her yard it was very evident that he was in the middle of it. There were pumpkins, gourds, and corn stalks everywhere, there was even a small parking lot just beyond her lawn. He knew that Grandma Betty and Clem were putting in long hours in the evenings since it opened, helping Zoey as much as possible. For now the yard was quiet as he walked through it to the field and road beyond.

The loud drone of the engines kept him walking in that direction. When he got past what he was convinced was a corn maze, he saw the combine at the other end of the field. Was Evie in there, was she thinking of Jasper? Yelling from the truck confirmed his suspicions. Evie had to be driving the combine while Zoey drove the truck.

Turning, he started in Zoey's way with a wave. She was actually sitting on the hood of the truck leaning against the windshield. Jasper didn't expect anything less, Charley was always getting after her for that same thing when she was younger. But there she was, sitting there looking at her phone without a care in the world. Just waiting for her sister to need her and to honk the horn on the combine.

He smiled up at the redhead as he climbed onto the hood and sat down next to her. She looked over at him and asked, "Are you ready for round two?"

"That's why I am here," he answered, knowing the real reason he was here was to see Evie. The appeal of harvesting corn had diminished as time had passed since his grandpa's death.

"Did Betty fill you in on what we are doing?" she asked, but she had already turned back to her phone.

"Are we not combining corn? First here, then at Grandma's house." It still felt weird not adding Grandpa to that.

"Nope," she said and typed something. When she was done, she said, "We work over here during the day and then move over to Betty's after three. That way you guys are not messing up my guests at the pumpkin patch."

"So you're not helping after three?" he asked. At least then Evie would have to talk to him if they had to work alone for hours a day.

She typed again and laughed at little to herself. "Nope, and we are binning it all. No trips to town. So, the person in the truck gets a little downtime."

"You mean so you can sext with your lover," he teased.

She let out a full laugh and pushed him with her elbow, as she said, "Yes."

"I'm glad you are happy, little Zoey," he said as he pulled her into a hug.

"Me too," she said, which was not the answer he was expecting. "And don't call me that name or I will have to kick your ass."

He laughed. She probably could since she had only left the Army six months ago. He put up his hands in surrender and said, "No fun nicknames. Okay?"

Sitting back, he watched the combine still in the distance. Here he was again, combining with Evie. He wondered if she thought of him when she was in there, of them.

"So, you're happy. What about her?" he couldn't help but ask. He needed to hear more about Evie, she was like a drug to him.

"She's good. The usual, I guess. You know Evie, she is all nurturing and calm, all even keel. Pretty bossy sometimes, but she is working on it," Zoey said. From beside him, he could see she was also looking at the combine. "Your grandpa's death really got to her, she hasn't really been herself since then. Something is different about her and I haven't figured it out yet. But I will."

"So when's the wedding?" he asked, changing the subject to avoid her finding out about him and Evie.

"Christmas. I have it all planned. Then we are going to spend January on our honeymoon," she answered.

"Where are you going?" he asked.

"Nowhere. Why?" She frowned in confusion.

"Where are you spending January then?" he asked.

"Mostly in my bedroom, with a little time spent in some other rooms in my house. Our house, I have to work on that," Zoey said with a smile.

"Don't you want to travel?" he asked. Most people went somewhere on their honeymoon.

"No, we've both been to a lot of places when we were in the military. Now we want to stay home." Zoey gestured expressively with her hands.

"Does sound more fun than traveling," Jasper agreed.

"And if I get on a plane, the minute I get off, that woman," she pointed at her sister who had turned the combine their way, "will stand in the airport surrounded by strangers holding signs to welcome me home. She's a little nuts."

"Why would she do that?" Such a gesture sounded more like Zoey than Evie.

"Because this last summer we got into a fight and I told her that I was hurt that she hadn't been there when I returned from Afghanistan. No one was there when I came home. And I wanted them there. Then Della and I went to Vegas for my birthday and when we got off the plane she was there, with Grandma Betty and Grandpa Bill, and the kids, and total strangers holding signs welcoming me back. It was amazing. She is amazing." Jasper could hear tears in her voice.

"She is amazing," he agreed, but he wasn't just talking about Evie's actions that day, he had always thought Evie was amazing.

"Greg messed her up pretty good, I think. Every few weeks some guy at the farmer's market will ask her out. She always says no. I wish she would just give someone a chance once in a while. She's not really happy, she deserves to be happy," Zoey said, as she looked out at the combine in the distance.

"It has been ten years. Do you even think she wants to get over him?" Jasper asked, needing to know the answer. A dead man was his only rival for Evie's heart, and the dead man was winning.

"It's not him, it's what he did, who he was. It was an awful marriage. I was here still. She isn't hiding her heart because she still loves him. I think it is because of how he treated her. She has no trust in anyone anymore. I need to figure out how to get her to trust again." Zoey pulled her legs up and rested her chin on her knees as she stared out at the combine in the distance.

"Maybe it's something she has to work through. Does she need your help?" Jasper wondered if Evie would actually take dating advice from her sister. Evie wasn't one for taking advice from anyone.

"Yes, she had ten years and didn't work it out. Now it is my turn," Zoey said with a smile.

"What if she is done with dating? Is she happy just farming and raising Ben?"

"No, I know she wants more. She is always excited about others getting married and having babies. She's a romantic," Zoey said.

"Evie? A romantic? The planner to the extreme?" Jasper said with some doubt.

"She is," Zoey agreed and then added, "She even got Gabe and I back together after a fight. And she doesn't even really like Gabe. Well, she likes him more now, but then she kind of hated him. She's so romantic."

A romantic, he thought as the combine swerved over to the truck to empty the hopper. He watched as it came closer and saw the moment Evie realized Jasper was with Zoey. He watched her gasp and wondered if she said his name.

Seeing how capable and in control Evie was, Jasper decided right then to do things differently. The next month he was going to pursue Evie with more romance than she knew what to do with. He would pursue her with everything he had. He just hoped it would be enough.

With just a month to convince her he was no longer a kid and that he could make her happy, he knew he had his work cut out for him.. A month to get her into bed with him again.

* * *

BUSINESS ONLY, that was all she would talk about with Jasper. She didn't think he would show up for corn harvest, but here he was. All sexy in jeans and a flannel shirt, no more shorts in the chilly autumn temperatures, but he looked good anyway. It had been a long three days since he had tried to touch her the last time they were alone, so since then she had made sure they were not alone.

Though she managed to stay put in the combine as Zoey and Jasper unloaded the corn into bins on Evie's farm, he had managed to corner her once in the shed. He had just touched her cheek, then he was gone. This morning he had climbed into the cab to tell her that he was going to bring Betty in for an appointment. After delivering his message, he had bent down and without touching her had whispered in her ear, "I like you driving barefoot better." Then was gone, but the words had made her toes curl in her tennis shoes.

Jasper and Zoey were palling around like they had in middle school so long ago. They were always laughing and fighting. Evie had once watched as Zoey flipped him onto the ground from a standing position. Evie had actually laughed when Jasper had pulled Zoey's leg out from under her and her little sister had hit the ground too. Then they scrambled up when they noticed she was heading their way with the combine.

Once Zoey abandoned them at three, she had forced either Clementine or Ben to help them in the field, though she knew they wanted to be at the pumpkin patched. With Jasper managing the truck alone, it took him longer to get back with each load, so there wasn't as much time for him to wait.

Today she would have brave it without one of the kids present. She had let them both go to the pumpkin patch after their nonstop begging. She just had to keep her guard up and stay away from the sexy man. But since he had shown up, she had formed a plan. Maybe his being around wouldn't be as bad as she had thought it was going to be. She had a proposition to run by him, just not yet. The plan was not fully there yet.

This morning Betty had called and said she wanted a meeting with everyone before the kids went to school. So, it was a little earlier in the morning that the entire group found themselves seated around Betty's table eating pancakes. Evie had ended up right next to Jasper, her leg actually touching his, and no room to move it away from him with everyone at the table.

"Can everyone be quiet?" Betty said. The older woman had not sat down to eat, just continued bringing more food to the table.

With her words, all present were suddenly silent. Forks were laid down, and all eyes were on the older woman. Evie felt Jasper touch her leg under the table. Her leg jerked at the touch, but his hand remained. And then he squeezed it. Suddenly, she was having a hard time breathing.

"I have decided, after talking to my sister Margery, to go on a vacation while Jasper is here to take care of Clem. Well, with the help of Evie and Zoey, of course. I know it might leave you short at the pumpkin patch, but I want to go before the snow comes. I have always wanted to go on an adventure." The older woman sounded like if anyone had an objection she would stay home. Betty was obviously happy when no one said anything.

All at the table offered encouragement. Everyone started talking at once.

"Where are you going?" Jasper asked.

"How long will you be gone?" Evie said

"Don't worry about the patch," Zoey stated.

Betty's eyes lit up with everyone's excitement. "We are going to the Grand Canyon and then drive on from there. We should only be gone for two or three weeks."

Jasper, who was still lightly rubbing Evie's leg, asked, "Driving?"

Betty smiled. "Margie has that camper and we are taking that. It will be quite the adventure. Your grandpa never wanted to leave this farm, now is my chance to see the world."

"When are you going?" Evie hoped she sounded like herself, Jasper's close contact and the leg rubbing was reminding her how good he was with his hands. Setting down her fork, she let her hand drop below the table, hoping no one noticed. Grabbing his hand, she moved it back to his own leg. Far away from her.

"This afternoon," Betty said and laughed. "We have to get going or I might change my mind."

"Okay, are you packed?" Jasper asked. The wayward hand was still trapped on his leg under her own. Slowly he slid his hand so that hers was sandwiched between his leg and his hand.

"I will be. Jasper, I want you to promise you will actually watch Clem and not just drop her off at Evie's. Evie has her hands full as it is. You have to do your part." The old lady was staring at them, sitting side by side. Could she tell Evie's wayward hand was trapped on his leg?

"I wouldn't do that to Evie," he said as if nothing was happening beneath the table. Slowly he moved her hand up his leg.

"Good, now, Zoey, are you going to be okay without me?" Betty's eyes left Jasper and Evie's and turned on Zoey.

Zoey was explaining how she would get by without Betty's help at the pumpkin patch when Jasper's hand brought hers up so high that she was cupping his erection, holding her hand there with his. With a slight move, he began to move his hand, so she was caressing his erection through his jeans. She could feel herself get beet red from the knowledge of what she was doing.

Pulling her hand away and jumping up, she mumbled, "I just

remembered something that I forgot to do this morning." Rushing over to Betty she gave her a hug, and said, "Have fun and don't worry about Clem." Then she was gone.

On the walk home she realized she had sounded like a moron, but it was the first—and only—excuse that had come to mind, so she went with it. She couldn't believe that Jasper had touched her below the table; that she had waited over six weeks for her to be able to touch *him*.

Once she made it into her house, she slammed the door shut and slid down to the floor. What was going on with her? In reality, she could have pulled her hand away at any time, she had just let it happen. Had she wanted to touch him like that? Yes, she had, she admitted.

Why was she suddenly sexually excited by a man? Why now after all these years? Why did it have to be Jasper that turned her on? When would she learn to control it?

CHAPTER 7

JASPER WAVED as his great aunt pulled out of the driveway with her RV, taking his grandmother on the adventure of her lifetime. He was excited for the older woman, because ever since he was a kid, he had heard her asking Grandpa Bill to go somewhere but he always said no. Jasper was sure that the only time his grandfather had ever set foot in the Minneapolis airport was the day he held the signs for Zoey when she came back from Vegas. He probably complained most of the way there too.

Now Jasper was in charge of a twelve-year-old girl for two to three weeks. Pretty vague timeline. But he knew with Evie would be there to help if things went south. She was great with the kids.

Evie, just her name made him happy. Her reaction during breakfast had told him everything he had been trying to figure out since he returned. At any time, she could have pulled her hand away, but she didn't. She wanted him as bad as he wanted her.

Now all he had to do was get her alone, not as easy of a task as he had originally thought. Between Zoey, the kids and harvest, he had only a few moments alone with her. He had tried to get Zoey to stay behind once when they had brought the corn and put it in the bin, but she had said if she stayed behind she would have to winterize the vegetable gardens and she would rather sit out in the field and do nothing. So, he hadn't been able to get Evie alone, and when he did, she ignored him.

He started walking across the road to Evie's, since the harvest had progressed to her property. Maybe he wouldn't have enough time for his project to romance Evie as he had thought he would. He just didn't have as much time as he had originally thought.

Walking past Evie's many gardens, he counted at least eight, but knew there were some he could not see. The one that drew his attention was across from the house. It drew his eyes whenever he was in her yard. The barn had been on that spot.

When he had been seventeen, he came home from a football game to find Evie and her husband, Greg's, barn on fire. Quickly he had pulled into the driveway, all his thoughts focused on the safety of the young couple. When no one answered the door with his pounding on the door, he panicked and with all his strength, broke down the front door. To this day he still didn't know why he had broken in. The house wasn't on fire. But he had to get inside. Running through the house, Jasper looked for the family but the house was empty, no Evie, no Greg, no baby Ben. He even looked in some less likely places to see if Greg had just passed out. Everyone knew he had a terrible drinking problem, he could have been passed out anywhere.

As a last resort, he had grabbed their phone and called Evie's dad who lived across the field. Relief had him sinking to the ground when Evie answered the phone. *She was alive*, was all his mind could process, *alive and safe*. He told her what was happening, and she told him to stay in the house.

But Jasper went outside after hanging up to watch her car speed into the yard. She stopped in front of the burning building.

Jumping out of the car she frantically yelled, "Have you seen Greg?"

His only answer had been to shake his head.

Both turned and looked at the burning barn at the same time, it had been Greg's preferred hang out since they had moved onto the farm. It was where he went to be alone and where he went to drink. Jasper was sure that since he wasn't in the house, that was where he was.

As did Evie it seemed. When she took off running toward the burning building, Jasper caught her before she made it to the door. Gabbing her by the waist he carried her away, all the fight gone out of her as she let him pull her away. They both knew that there was nothing they could do. Greg was already gone.

Within minutes the firetrucks showed up. Three trucks came and every cop in the county. He and Evie had sat on the front step of her house watching the action silently. Neither knew what to say, what to do.

When the police chief and the fire chief walked to the door, Jasper grabbed her hands in his. They told her they had found Greg Singleton in the barn, drunk maybe. Jasper later heard that he had shot himself after lighting the fire. When Evie had heard the news, she had no reaction. She did not cry, nor did she scream.

Charley came and got her and brought her back to his place. Jasper went home and wondered what had actually happened that night. Evie and Ben had been at Charley's in the middle of the night and Greg had killed himself while alone at their house.

All Jasper felt was relieved and happy that Evie was free from the man. In the short time they had been married the man had alienated himself from everyone on either side of the road. Now Jasper no longer had to worry about Evie living alone with him.

Jasper had known that Greg had been abusive, but nobody had ever called him on it. A week before the fire he had even thought that he had beaten Zoey. Due to their poor relationship she wouldn't confirm or deny that it had happened after the fire. But Jasper had seen the bruises at the funeral. The man drank to excess and beat women, Jasper had been a little glad he was dead.

During the funeral, Grandma Betty had agreed to watch baby Ben. But Jasper had told her he would watch the baby so she could go. What he didn't tell her was that he would not go and mourn the man who had made Evie's life hell. He had stayed with the toddler and played with the boy. He had explained that his dad was also a jerk, they had that in common.

The next spring, he and Grandpa Bill had cleaned up the area and Evie had planted her first garden on the spot. From those ashes, she had built her business. By the time Jasper had left for college, he some-times forgot that Evie had been married. To this day he had a hard time believing she was a widow, or that she had never remarried. He couldn't believe there was not a man in the area that didn't think she was gorgeous. He was starting to understand that there were men interested, but it was Evie who was not.

Getting to the edge of the field he headed to the parked truck. As he walked, he watched the combine already making its way down the field, Evie was in the machine every chance she got. He figured she was mostly avoiding him. Which made it even more surprising when he saw her sitting on the hood of the truck. He smiled and thought Zoey must be wearing off on her a little.

"Grandma Betty's off on her great adventure." He climbed up on the hood of the old truck with her.

"Good," she said, but didn't look up from the papers she was looking at. She started leafing through a yellow notebook and then stopped and wrote something on the paper in front of her.

He looked over her shoulder. "What are you doing?"

"Finances, I've been too busy to get them done. Since you and Zoey were able to screw around so much during the day, I thought I could get some of this done," she said, returning the pencil to her mouth.

He sat back and watched her, just enjoying the view. She looked through her yellow notebook and then wrote down a number in the ledger in front of her. Then did it again, and again. The pencil always returning to her mouth for safekeeping.

"Don't you have all this on a computer?" he asked.

She looked up and through the pencil in her mouth she said, "No."

"Why not?" he asked.

"I can't do computer work out here," she said, then took the pencil out and wrote a number.

"There are laptops, Hart," he said. Today she was wearing a gray flannel shirt that opened to reveal a black tank top below it. Her jeans were tight fitting and hugged her curves. The tank top did not hide the fact that she was not wearing a bra today. Again.

"Singleton, not Hart. Laptops cost money," she said.

"Not that much." He watched her concentrate on her task.

"I'd have to find a computer program that works for me," she said, once again flipping through her yellow notebook.

"You could have asked me. I am an accountant," he said.

"I never thought of it," she admitted with a half-smile. Then went back to looking through her papers.

"Can I look at your papers? Maybe I know of a program off the top of my head that you can use." He took the papers from her and looked at them. The information on the pages meant nothing to him. Only Evie knew what everything meant. He was not going to decipher this code.

He looked through the notebook again and then reached over and took the pencil from her mouth. She let it go and he wrote a word on the top of the first page. She looked at it and asked, "What is that?"

"That is the program I am going to buy for you. I'll get all this information into the program and teach you how to use it. You can't keep doing it this way, not now that you have Zoey working for you too," he explained, circling the word he had written.

"I can do it myself. It's not some big company," she defended herself and trying to grab back the papers he was holding.

"Stop being stupid. Say thank you, Jasper," he said as he organized her paperwork in a pile.

"I can do it myself," she repeated.

"Keep up your arguing and I will get you a laptop, too," he said. She reached for her papers, but he kept them out of her reach.

"I don't need your help," she hissed.

"You get a laptop now, say thank you, Jasper."

She stopped trying to get her papers back and folded her arms.

"Evie, how many times were you there to help my grandparents when I wasn't around? Or even when I was? Me buying you a computer and a program is a drop in the bucket compared to what I owe you for being there for them. Money can't buy the friendship you have given them. I owe you so much and most will never get payed back. Let me do this for you."

She looked away from him into the distance for a long time. He wanted to touch her, drag her into his arms. But knew that would make her even madder at him. Without turning back to him she said, "Thank you, Jasper."

He placed the papers on her lap and she grabbed them up close to her chest. Quickly she climbed off the hood of the truck and started to walk away when he called to her. "Where are you going?"

She turned still holding the paper to her chest. "You can handle this today. I am going to work on this at home." She turned again and walked away.

Appreciating the view as she walked away, he wondered if he had just made things worse between them. You never knew with Evie, were they getting closer or further from each other?

* * *

Evie sat at her kitchen table looking over the papers that she had fought Jasper over. They were scattered around and were not making sense to her today. She hated doing the books. She hated to admit that numbers were not her friend. They tended to make no sense at all.

His nice words about her had nearly made her cry. She hadn't been friends with his grandparents for years for any other reason than that she loved them. That he appreciated her for that made her choke up.

Knowing that Jasper was right about the computer program thing didn't make Evie any more inclined to admit it. After trying a few different programs she had never found one that worked for her operation. Since Zoey had joined the farm this year things would have to change, but Evie was having a hard time letting that change actually happen.

Looking out the window, her mind went through a list of things she could be doing on the farm. But as Jasper driving the truck came into the yard to unload a load of corn into the bin, she decided there were a lot of things to do inside also. Working on finances wasn't the worst task around.

She was not avoiding Jasper. Okay, she was totally avoiding Jasper. He got under her skin, made her want things she hadn't wanted in a long time. Things she definitely didn't need, she decided.

When her front door opened, she knew it would be Jasper since she hadn't heard the truck leave the yard. Not looking up when he walked into the kitchen, Evie continued to ignore him when he sat in the chair across from her. When his butt hit the seat, she pulled all the papers toward her. No way was he getting her papers from her again.

"Evie, I'm sorry about what happened. I shouldn't have been pushy about the accounting stuff. It's just that's what I know. I am an accountant. I can help you get this stuff straightened out." He pointed at the papers that she was holding down with her arms.

His words made her looked up at him. "I'm sorry I never thought to ask you for help."

"I don't know why you would have asked. I haven't really been around," he admitted. Sadness showed in his brown eyes.

"I didn't ask because of Della," she admitted. Then quickly explained, "Della is a corporate attorney, she can't help me with legal stuff, she doesn't deal in little stuff. You work at a big accounting firm, you deal in big business stuff, not a little business stuff. Does that make sense?"

"It does." He grabbed hold of her hand still laying on the table.

She stared at their hands and sighed. "Zoey and I hired another attorney. One that is not Della. She insisted on us using someone else. Conflict of interest."

"I'm still going to help you with this. I ordered the stuff and it will be here tomorrow. I will help you get it set up," he said, rubbing his thumb over the back of her hand.

"But I don't need you to do that for me," she stated stubbornly. Over the years she had learned not to rely on anyone, she did it for herself or it didn't get done. It was hard to let go of that control.

"I want to help you, Evie. Can you accept my help?" Jasper asked.

"I guess," she said quietly.

"You spend all your time helping others, sometimes you need help too. Let me help you." He squeezed her hand, got up and walked back out the door. Evie had been able to keep the tears at bay until the door shut behind him, but once it slammed shut, they poured out. He made her sound so selfless, so much better than she was.

CHAPTER 8

JASPER WAS SURPRISED the next day when only Zoey showed up to begin work. Was Evie still avoiding him? At close to three, Evie finally came out and switched places with Zoey, so she could get the pumpkin patch ready. Evie had been quiet, not saying much in the next four hours they worked together. When the day was over, she drove the combine into the Reed's shed and walked home without a word. He wanted to go with her, but after a day of trying to talk to her and failing he was sure she wouldn't talk to him now.

Now she was a no-show for another day, or at least the morning shift. He didn't realize how much he liked to watch her walk up his driveway in the morning until she wasn't there. They always started at the Reed's shed because his grandfather had built a shed big enough for the combine years ago. Neither Evie nor Zoey had a building big enough for it on their properties.

"Good morning, Jasper," Zoey called out.

"Where is your lovely sister?" he asked as Zoey drew near.

"Della will be here later today, to help me this evening." Zoey winked at him.

"How about the blond one, the one that likes to boss you around?" he asked as they headed to the shed.

"Minneapolis," she said. "I thought you knew. It's Saturday, farmer's market day. She left hours ago with the kids. One of them under your supposed care."

"I guess I forgot." Jasper had no idea. Evie hadn't said anything the day before. The kids had wanted a sleepover and he had said Clem could go. He did not know that would lead to Evie taking the kid into the city.

"Don't be mad she took the kids, during pumpkin season she needs extra hands to haul the pumpkins in and out of the trailer. She'll be sore as it is when she gets back. I know I always am. That's why I leave my pumpkins in the field and let others pick them up," Zoey said and laughed.

"Smart," Jasper agreed, wondering if there was any way Evie would let him give her a back rub tonight. The chances were pretty low, but he would keep his eyes out for her return.

The sun was hot and high in the sky when he watched a familiar woman walking out to the field from Evie's yard from his spot on the hood of the truck. He couldn't help but smile, but as she drew close, he realized it was not Evie, just another Hart sister.

It had always amazed him how alike the sisters were in stature and the way they moved. If you didn't know them well, it was hard to tell them apart at a distance. Up close, it was easy. Della was more confident and it showed in her posture and manners. Zoey was upbeat and bouncy. Evie was … Evie. She seemed to be more confident than Zoey and more upbeat then Della. She balanced them out.

He waved Della over to the truck. He noticed she was wearing perfectly tailored jeans and a nice leather jacket when she got close enough. Her shoes looked like they were meeting dirt for the first time in their lives and not enjoying it. A perfect outfit for a lawyer to attend an evening in a suburban backyard. Not really appropriate for walking through a dirty field.

"Afternoon, Della," Jasper said. He was about to jump down from his seat on the truck when she climbed up beside him, surprising him. Her outfit probably cost more than the truck they were sitting on, but she didn't seem to mind sitting on the dirty rusty metal.

"Jasper, how is it going?" she asked as she pulled a hair elastic from her pocket and pulled her medium length, straight brown hair into a ponytail. He almost laughed at the oldest Hart sister, her hair was naturally as red and curly as Zoey's but she obviously had worked hard to tame it. He was secretly glad that Evie had left her hair alone.

"Good," he said. He and Della had not really had a conversation in years. At two years older than Evie, Della was almost seven years older than him. By the time he was an adult she had already become a high-power attorney in Minneapolis. And neither had seemed to return to Birch Cove at the same time.

The opposite of Evie, who had had a baby before she could legally drink, Della had graduated from high school three years early and was an attorney before her sister's baby had even been born. Though taking different paths in life, the sisters seemed close.

He watched as she looked out at the cornfield. She was watching Zoey run the combine as she asked, "Grandma Betty says you work downtown?"

"Yes. You?" he asked her.

"Yes, do you live down there?" she asked.

"Yes, about six blocks from my office. How about you?" he asked.

She laughed, and he heard Zoey's laugh in hers. "No, thank you. I will save my money. I live in the burbs in an apartment."

"It is expensive in the city," he agreed.

"And getting worse. I am saving my money for a house, but until then it's cheap little places for me," she said.

"And clothes?" Jasper looked her up and down as she had clearly spent a mint on the outfit she was wearing.

She laughed again and leaned back on the windshield, reminding him of Zoey doing the same thing. "No need, I have the perfect body for clearance racks. Short with little feet. I have never paid full price for clothes."

He leaned back and looked at the combine progress and asked, "Do you help out here a lot?"

"I used to more. With Zoey back, I am not needed as much. I usually help with the farmer's market in Minneapolis, but this year Zoey was here for that. So, they just stayed at my place and I didn't have to spend the days in the sun. But with Betty gone, Zoey asked if I could help with the pumpkin patch tonight. She didn't want Evie and the kids to spend the day in Minneapolis and then have to help her all evening." Della pulled out her phone and looked at it as she talked.

"Evie spreads herself a little thin, I have noticed," Jasper agreed.

"A little, she looked like crap this morning when I stopped at the market. They didn't stay with me last night. She drove in early this morning. She needs more help out here, more than Zoey even." Della voiced the same worry Jasper was thinking.

They sat in silence watching Zoey drive the giant combine toward them. Zoey pulled into position and then jumped out of the cab. Della slid off the truck hood and ran to her sister, and he watched as they hugged in greeting.

They both turned and walked to him and he had to suppress a grin, they were the exact same height and build, they could have been twins even if there was a six year age gap between them. The obvious difference between them was their attire: Della wore expensive clothes and as Zoey was more comfortable in old jeans and a flannel shirt. They even had the same walk, Evie's walk.

Zoey spoke for them both when she said, "We are leaving you. You can take care of all this."

He laughed and said, "Go ahead. I can live without you both."

Della laughed at his joke and added, "But you will miss us like crazy."

And since he had slid off the truck, they enveloped him in a group hug and then left the field.

Jasper spent the next three hours both combining and hauling the corn. It was harder than he had originally thought it would be when he had told Evie he didn't need her help. Now he didn't know how he could have done it with her. Or even if he wanted to do the harvest if she was not there.

After he had gotten everything in the shed for the night, he looked at Evie's yard to see if her truck was there. His heart did a flip when he saw that it was, but he also saw that Della's fancy SUV was parked next to it. He could hear music playing in the distance and walked up his grandmother's driveway to see where it was coming from. Once he made it to the road, he realized it was coming from Zoey's house.

Unable to stop himself from going over to see what was going on, his feet took him down the road to Zoey's and the party that seemed to be going on. Evie might be there. He had gotten used to seeing her every day, and today he hadn't gotten his fix today. Yet.

* * *

EVIE WAS EXHAUSTED, but both her sisters were sitting by the firepit talking, so she joined them. The farmer's market had been busy as usual, and even with two young helpers she had been busy all day. She had sent the kids for lunch and by the time she had gotten to eat the hotdog they had brought back it was cold, but she ate it anyway. It had been disgusting and had made her a little queasy for the rest of the afternoon.

Watching the fire, she let the conversation flow around her. Wedding plans were basically all Zoey and Della were talking about. She loved her baby sister, but she couldn't always talk about wedding stuff.

"Are you listening, Evie?" Della asked.

"Yes," Evie said.

"What did I say?" Zoey demanded.

"I can't remember," Evie admitted as she stared into the fire.

Della dragged her chair closer to Evie's. "You have to slow down. You will get sick."

Evie shook her head. "I am fine, don't worry about me."

"I have to. You don't worry about you, so I have to," Della insisted.

"I'm fine. I just have a lot on my mind right now. In a month, I can slow down for a few months," Evie said. Winters were when she had nothing to do. It was the time she got caught up on sleep and other things.

"Zoey, you have to give her a day off once in a while," Della told her sister.

"I can try, but you know her." Arguing with their oldest sister Zoey moved her chair close to Evie's other side and said, "Switching topics: Evie has the dreaded curls."

Evie watched as both sisters touched her newly cut hair. She had needed a change, had for a few months, but had finally gotten the courage after the farmer's market to cut half of her hair off. She had had long hair for so long she couldn't remember not having it. But the work it involved was getting on her nerves, so she went for it. It was still longer than both of her sisters, but it was a drastic change for Evie. When the stylist had turned her around in the chair, she saw that the blond locks were curling at the ends. After getting home she showered, and all she saw was Zoey and Della's curls on her head, just a different color. It would take some getting used to.

"I can't believe it either. I never knew," Evie said touching her hair. "Now I look just like you, too."

The sisters laughed at their shared hair issues.

Della sat back in her chair, "I have an announcement."

"A man?" Zoey asked.

"God forbid, no," Della stated, "I was fired this week."

Evie sat up, instantly awake. "Aren't you up for partner?"

"Not anymore," Della stated flatly.

"Why?" Zoey asked.

"Fraternization," Della said.

"Because of that guy at the office you were seeing?" Zoey asked, last spring Della had a relationship with a man she worked with. Neither of the sisters had ever seen him or even heard what his name was.

"Yes. So now I am jobless. And I won't get a letter of recommendation which will make finding a new one almost impossible," Della explained tossing her empty plastic cup into the fire.

Evie was surprised that Della wasn't more upset about the situation. She had worked for the same firm since she graduated from law school over ten years ago. Though she had to work a lot of hours, she had always seemed to love it. Maybe she was just in shock about the situation.

"Yayyy," Evie said with a smile and both her sisters looked at her.

"You're happy she got fired? You're such a good sister," Zoey said dryly.

"I just mean, now she can move back here. She can open her own law firm and help all the woman in this town who are getting screwed over in their divorces," Evie explained.

"I am a corporate lawyer," Della reminded her.

"You're a lawyer and you can do anything," Evie said.

"So what? I just to rent a place downtown?" Della leaned back in her chair, ready to pick apart Evie's suggestion.

"No, you are going to open it in the Connor Mansion. I have the deed at the house, it's already yours." The Connor Mansion was their maternal grandparent's house in town. It wasn't like Evie hadn't dreamed of this moment for years and planned Della's return home. Evie would never overstep like that—much.

The house has been empty for most of the girl's lives, but it was still in great shape. Every time Evie went in to check on it she thought that they should sell it if they were not going to use it, but she hated for it to be out of the family.

"I am not moving into that place, it's falling down," Della said. Evie knew full well the house had not been lived in for thirty years.

"We will get it fixed," Evie said.

"I have to think about this. I have one more place to check before I throw in the towel on my career," Della said.

But Evie wasn't listening because she had just heard Gabe yell out Jasper's name, inviting him to join them.

She stayed where she was, too tired to do anything else. Zoey jumped up and offered to get him something to eat. Both kids swarmed him, talked to him for a little and then ran off. He finally walked toward her and said, "Evening, Evie, Della." Then he sat in the seat beside Evie that Zoey had just left.

Evie was powerless to do anything but stay in the chair she was in and let the conversations flow around her. Jasper asked Della about restaurants in Minneapolis and Gabe and Zoey joined in. Jasper ate as the conversation turned to people everyone knew, or at least most of them knew. And Evie just let the conversation and the familiar voices lull her into sleep.

"Evie, wake up," Jasper was saying as she woke up.

She sat up and all eyes were on her. "I wasn't asleep," she protested.

"I'll walk her home," Jasper said. "Della, can you bring the kids home when they are ready to go?"

Everyone seemed to agree she needed to go home and that Jasper would be the one to walk her there. She was too tired to protest the plan. She let him escort her away from her family as they all called goodbye to them.

They were halfway down Zoey's driveway before Evie said, "I can get home on my own."

"Can you? You look about ready to pass out. In fact, you did back there," Jasper said and took her hand in his as they walked in the dark.

"You can't pass out when you haven't been drinking," she said, but she didn't let his hand go. She was enjoying the innocent touch of her hand in his.

"When you can't stay awake to talk to your sisters, it's passing out," he said.

"I have been tired lately, that's all," Evie explained. Getting up before dawn today for the farmer's market had not helped.

Neither spoke as they turned onto the gravel road. When they were halfway to their joint driveways Jasper said, "You cut your hair."

"Yes, it was getting in the way all the time," she explained.

"I liked it long, it's beautiful with the curls, but I liked how sometimes it would touch me. At the funeral, it made me forget I was burying my grandfather when I could feel it. And of course, when we made love, I couldn't get enough of it," he stopped and lifted her hand to his mouth for a kiss.

Trying to pull away from him, his words both scared her and excited her at the same time. Chalking it up to being too tired to be having this conversation she said, "Let's not talk about that, please. I can't deal with it today."

"We need to one day, Evangelina Hart." He kissed her hand again.

"Singleton," she corrected.

He stopped her in the middle of the road and grabbed her other hand and said, "I don't ever want to think of you connected with that bastard. I know you still love him for some reason, but I don't. You have and will always be a Hart in my mind."

"Why do you think I still love him?" she asked in confusion.

He lifted her hand to his mouth again and said, "Because you still wear his ring." He lowered her hands and then dropped them. "Goodnight, Evie, please get some sleep."

She watched as he walked away, then turned and headed toward her house in the dark. She touched the ring he had mentioned and twisted it. She had been wearing it so long she didn't even notice it anymore. Maybe it was time to take it off.

Heading up the stairs to her bedroom she wondered if she shouldn't have changed her name back to Hart years ago. Was she hiding behind Greg's memory? Was she keeping the world at bay with a gold ring? Changing into her pajamas she climbed into bed. But before she shut the light off, she took her ring off and placed it on the bedside table.

The gold glistened in the light as it lay, lonely, on the wooded surface. Her dad had given it to Greg to give her on their wedding day. Greg hadn't even gotten a ring for her. It had been her Grandma Connor's before belonging to her.

She had to admit she didn't even think about Greg when she noticed it. She thought about her grandparents sitting on their front porch holding hands well into old age. It was the only memory she had of the older couple that had passed away when she was six. It was what she always thought what marriage would be. But it was not the kind of marriage she had gotten herself into. Nor had it been the kind of marriage her parents had. But it was what she had always longed for. It was the kind of marriage her sister was getting. She could see that. Just watching her future brother-in-law look at her baby sister, she knew that theirs was that kind of love.

Maybe one day she would find that for herself. But Evie doubted it, because she was afraid she was losing her heart to Jasper. Jasper who would be gone again in two weeks. And he would take her heart with him when he left.

Shutting the light off, she left the ring on the side table. She didn't feel any different now that it was off. She was the same Evie as she had been before, just without a ring on.

CHAPTER 9

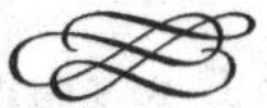

SUNDAY STARTED off dark and rainy. It was the first time it had rained since he had come to town a week and a half before. He was looking forward to not being in the field all day. He was a little disappointed when the morning rains cleared up and the sun came out. Tomorrow, it seemed they would be back to work.

He sent a text to Evie to see if she was home midmorning, but she had responded that she was not. Noticing that only Della's little SUV was in front of Evie's house, Jasper deduced that Della was with her somewhere. He decided he had better do laundry while he could, because soon both he and Clem would be out of clean clothes.

Clem had stayed in her room all day. She had ventured out for lunch and then crawled back in. Midafternoon she came out and asked, "Can I go to Evie and Ben's?"

"They're not home." Folding the last load of laundry, he had gotten it all done.

"Yes, they are." She complained, "Why won't you let me go over there?"

His head shot up with confusion. "I am fine with you going over there, just not if they are not home."

Her eyes rolled at him. "Ben just texted, they are there."

He stopped folding, "Fine, let's go over there."

"You don't have to go." She headed for the door.

"I am going with and you'll wait for me," Jasper yelled as the door slammed shut after her as she left the house.

Throwing the laundry back into the basket he grabbed the box that was sitting by the door and headed across the road. He was excited to see Evie, even if he knew that she would probably be mad about the computer.

As he made his way down Evie's driveway, he saw that Della was putting her luggage in her SUV.

"Hi," he said when she noticed him.

"Hi, what's in the box?" she asked.

"Computer and software for the farm," he explained.

"Good, Evie gets nailed at tax time for her bad bookkeeping. Better teach both her and Zoey how to run it. Evie can fix that combine but can't run a computer to save her life. And I don't think Zoey is much better about it." Della shut her trunk.

She walked into the house with him and yelled, "Jasper is here to save the farm."

Both sisters were in the living room. Zoey yelled, "Finally!"

"We don't need saving," Evie said calmly from her spot on the couch.

"What's in the box?" Ben asked.

Showing Ben the computer, he started to set it up as he watched the sisters hug goodbye at the door. He had never noticed that they were such big huggers until Grandpa Bill's funeral. Now he realized that they hugged hello and goodbye each time one of them came or went.

When Della had left the yard, the kids had gone up to Ben's room, and Zoey had gone to the kitchen for something to eat, Jasper asked Evie, "When did you guys start hugging? I don't remember that much hugging before."

She looked at him over her coffee cup. Her hair was in a braid today and her yellow shirt made her eyes greener than usual. "When Zoey came home last spring, I started to hug her every chance I got. I think she had a little PTSD. Since then I haven't quit and Della and

Zoey have started to hug more also. It is really nice, makes you feel loved."

She was smiling, he could tell without even looking up. When he did, he smiled back at her. "I should try that more too. You gave me the best hug at the funeral. I should have known you had been practicing."

"Practicing what?" Zoey came into the living room with a bag of chips in her hands.

"Evie hugging," was all Jasper said.

"Yeah, she has turned us all into huggers. Sometimes I even hug her when I come to work in the morning. I can't help it." Zoey laughed at her sister and gave her a quick hug before sitting in the chair across from Evie on the couch.

Evie lowered the cup and said, "Notice that she's the one hugging me when she gets to work, not me hugging her. I've just chalked it up to being in love."

"Where is Gabe today?" Jasper asked.

Zoey ate a chip and said, "Sleeping. He is on nights this week. He took off a few hours last night since Della was coming home."

Jasper nodded. "Where is your paperwork, Evie? I have a few things to do before I show you guys how to do this, but I need to look over your stuff first."

He spent the entire afternoon getting the computer set up and showing both women how to use it. It had only taken a few minutes to realize neither were very computer savvy—neither of them even wanted to learn to use it. Zoey had begged him more than once to do their books for them. She had zoned out early and started to find excuses to leave the room. He had counted at least seven bathroom breaks and four snack breaks. Evie sat through it all but wasn't paying much attention to the accounting program he had gotten them. But the second program made especially for farmers caught her attention immediately. Using the program, she could enter how many plants she planted versus how much she sold.

Zoey left just before five, leaving Jasper and Evie alone for the first time that day. He worried she would be nervous to be alone with him, but Evie acted like he wasn't even in the room. He wandered into the kitchen and started a frozen lasagna for them all for supper.

He wandered back into the living room, realizing that Evie hadn't moved. He watched her, wishing her fingers were on him instead of the keypad.

"What did you guys do this morning?" He had no right to ask. But he wanted to know what she did all day. To know what she did when he wasn't around.

She looked up and blinked at him. "What?"

"What did you guys do this morning?" he repeated.

"Church and then we looked at the mansion," she said as if she looked at a mansion every day.

"What mansion?" he asked.

"Mine." She was trying to pay attention to both the computer and him. But the computer was winning.

"You have a mansion?" He had known her his entire life and had never heard of this.

"Yes." She didn't look up.

"Where?" He moved until he saw her eyes, but they were glued to the screen.

"In town." Still her eyes didn't leave the screen.

"Birch Cove?" he asked.

"Yes." Her green eyes flashed across the screen and she smiled a little at it.

"Why?" He didn't even know if she knew what she was saying.

"Della might move back and open a law firm from it."

"Why would she do that?" he asked, still wondering how she had a mansion in the first place.

She looked up at him and finally pushed the computer away. "Because she loves this town and wants to help its people in legal matters."

"Are we talking about the same woman who walked through a cornfield with thousand dollar shoes?" He had seen them when she left and they were muddy and probably destroyed.

"Probably. I don't know what she pays for shoes, but she has a lot of them."

"I don't see her leaving behind her six-figure salary for small town lawyering," Jasper said.

"You don't know her well," Evie stated.

"I think you're projecting your wants onto her," he said.

"I am not." She bristled at his suggestion. "She just has to change the plan she has been following her entire life."

"Let's just drop why she is moving back and talk about this mansion you own. What else do you own?" he asked, trying to avoid her getting mad at him again today.

"Just this house and the mansion, but I am hoping Della wants it. Oh, and Zoey's house. That is in the trust also," she said as her fingers inched toward the laptop.

"All of this is in a trust?" he asked. He was surprised that he had never heard of it before. Maybe his grandparents didn't know.

"Yes, Della set it up after Dad died. She said it would be better since I was the only one around here. It's worked out pretty well, I rent the land from the trust and the trust pays all the taxes." She had the computer in front of her again.

"Do I know the mansion?" he asked.

"I don't know. It's the Connor Mansion, do you know of it?" He was losing her to the computer again.

"Yes, the giant house that takes up over half a block just off Main Street. It's haunted," he said.

"It's not haunted. It's just empty. Dad rented it out once, and they painted over some of the woodwork but since then it's been empty. Grandma and Grandpa left the house to us girls," she concluded, her eyes glued to the computer screen.

He sat back in the chair and watched her type. He was enjoying the faces she kept making at the machine as she worked. Did she even realize that she was making them? Every once in a while, she would say a word or two to herself, mostly yes, no, and some muttered really's.

Pulling himself away, he went to finish getting supper ready for Evie and the kids. It was a different experience making a meal for a woman and two kids. He was excited to see what she said when she found out he had cooked for her. He didn't have to wait long to find out because as he heated up garlic bread she came in to help.

"Thanks for starting something, it slipped my mind." She grabbed plates from the cabinet.

"You were too excited about your new computer," Jasper teased, taking the plates from her.

She turned and grabbed glasses and she said, "Maybe I was a little into the computer."

"I am glad you like it, Hart." He placed the plates on the table and watched as she placed the glasses next to them. He smiled when she looked up at him and she smiled back. She didn't correct him about her name this time. Maybe things were going his way.

CHAPTER 10

EVIE PLACED the last of the dishes in the dishwasher as she stalled for time. Tonight was the night she was going to ask Jasper for a big favor while the kids were busy playing video games upstairs. If she didn't do it tonight she would chicken out. Closing the door on the dishwasher, she headed to the living room where Jasper ended up after dinner.

She found him on the couch working on her new computer. Could he be any nicer? She still had no idea if she would use it, for accounting at least. His little program about marketing her products was fun.

Casually she tried to sit on the other side of the couch from him, but bumped her elbow on the edge of the couch instead. *Smooth, Evie. Very graceful.* She rubbed it, hoping he didn't notice.

He looked over at her. "I am just entering more numbers in the finance program so you don't have to."

"Thanks," she said, rubbing her elbow.

"Did you buy this couch? It is very uncomfortable." He touched the fancy arms with wood inlay.

"No, Della bought it, but it didn't fit in her apartment, so she's letting me use it until she gets a bigger place. If she does move into the mansion, I'll have to buy all new stuff because most of this stuff is hers."

"I can tell. Della is not afraid to spend her money," he observed.

"She makes it, she can spend it," Evie said. It had never bothered her, Della was high maintenance, but she maintained herself.

"I guess," he said, typing a few more numbers.

"Are the kids upstairs?" she asked, eyeing the stairway across the room.

"Yeah."

"Can we talk?" she asked hoping he would say no so she wouldn't have to embarrass herself. She shouldn't have asked because he of course would talk to her. And agree with her request, but only because he was a nice person.

He shut the computer and placed it on the coffee table in front of him. He turned toward her and smiled. "I have been waiting to talk to you since I got back, since I left maybe. I never realized how good at avoiding conversations you were."

"It's not about that," she said trying to keep her volume down. But she was nervous and felt her voice was loud, too loud. "Well, it's a little about that."

"Good," he said.

"Keep your voice down," she said, looking at the stairway again.

"Do you want to talk somewhere more private?" he asked. "Like your bedroom?"

She snapped her head up to face him. "You mean the room across from Ben's? Real private." She got up and motioned him to follow, she didn't wait to see if he did. She walked to the laundry room that was off the kitchen and hoped he would follow. When he did, she closed the door behind him.

Maybe this was too private, she thought. Maybe it was too small. He was right there, she had no place to go to get away from him. She felt his hands on her hips as he lifted her onto the washing machine. Once she was sitting on top, they were eye level. Even closer. Even worse.

"Nice and private. Now we can talk," he said looking at her face, his hands still on her waist. His clever hands had actually found their way underneath her shirt and were resting on the bare skin just above the waist of her jeans. His hands were a distraction.

She blushed and rubbed her hands over her face. "I cannot look at you and talk to you. Turn around."

Pulling his hands from her skin, she watched as he dramatically pouted and turned away from her. Now she could only see his strong back right at fingertip distance. Her fingers inched to touch him.

"Okay, I'm not facing you," he said, she could tell he was trying not to laugh.

"Now I'm going to talk and you are going to listen. No talking until I say so. Agreed?" she demanded from behind him.

"Yes, but I hope that not all our private conversations are like this, Hart. I kind of like to see you when we talk. Since we do it so little." She could tell he was smiling as he said it.

"No talking." She started to chicken out. What was she going to say? How was he going to react?

As if sensing her reticence, he remained silent and she closed her eyes so she didn't have to look at his back. His gray T-shirt was stretched across his broad shoulders, making her want to touch him. Taking a deep breath she said, "I want to ask you a favor. Don't say anything until you know what it is. You can nod if you agree."

She knew he would nod she didn't have to open her eyes to see it, because he was too nice and would do almost anything for her. But would he agree to this? Well, she was about to find out.

"I have decided that I want to start dating, I want to find someone who looks at me like Gabe looks at Zoey. I want that kind of love. But in order to find that man I need to date. I might need to date a lot. I don't even know if that kind of guy would like me."

She continued, her eyes still closed. "At this point in my life I am very uncomfortable dating anyone. You see, I am a widow and that brings a lot of ideas to a man's head. The big one is sex, that I've had a lot of sex and am good at it. But I've only been with one man in my life, well, two counting you, and I am not good at sex." She felt his back tense at her words as if he wanted to contradict her confession but she barreled on. "With the other man—not you—well, it wasn't good. I know it was my fault. I've never known how to get good at sex. But you're *really* good at it. Really good. So … so … I would like you to teach me how to be good at sex."

She opened her eyes to find his warm brown eyes staring back at her. He had turned around. *Damn him!*

His hands were on either side of her, but he was not actually touching her. His dark eyes were so close she could see gold flecks that she had never noticed before. His gravelly voice said just above a whisper, "Yes. When?"

Her heart fluttered and her breath caught in her throat. He was going to do it. "Thank you, Jasper."

"Today?" his voice sounded off.

"No, the kids are here," she said as if stating the obvious.

"When?" He was so close she could feel his warm breath on her face.

"This week. Tuesday thru Friday during the day. If it rains," Evie had practiced the exact conversation in her head a hundred times, it had never gone this well. Mostly because he always said no when she was practicing.

"Very specific. Why then?" His forehead touched hers, the only part of their bodies touching.

"The kids are in school." She was having trouble breathing with him so close. "Gabe is off work, and if it rains, Zoey will stay home."

"Tell me it's going to rain one of those days," he said, as breathless as she felt.

"Most of them," she said.

"I can't wait to start the lessons."

"Lessons?" she asked. "Was I was really so terrible at it, it will take more than one?" Pulling away, she pushed him until she could slide off the washing machine and headed out of the room. She was so embarrassed she thought her performance had been at least okay. But now she knew the truth and couldn't face him.

He grabbed her arm and was about to say something when they heard the kids coming running from the upstairs. She opened the door to see Clem head out the front door and Ben running behind her, yelling, "You are acting crazy today."

Jasper said behind her, "I have to go. I will talk to you later about that."

And she watched him rush out after his cousin, following her back to their grandparent's house.

Watching her son stomp back up the stairs and slam the door behind him, she wondered if she had made a huge mistake. If she was that bad at sex that it would take more than one time, why would he even agree to it? Why would he want to do it again with her?

Pushing the uncertainty from her brain, she grabbed the computer and headed to her bedroom. She changed into her pajamas and sat in bed, not looking at the computer but looking out the window into the night. What had she done?

* * *

Jasper watched Zoey walk up the driveway to his grandmother's Tuesday morning, alone. It really only took two people to get the combine and the truck across the road, but both sisters usually came over in the morning. Not today. Just Zoey, and he was already in a bad mood when the sun came up. No rain in the forecast in what should have been day one of the favor.

Monday had turned into another full day of Evie avoiding Jasper, by now he should have been used to it. He had been unable to talk to her alone at all. Even after Zoey left at three, Evie had insisted Ben had to help her in the fields. Watching her all day, she hadn't even looked his way once. All day she had joked and laughed with her sister, but said nothing to him.

He knew the moment he said lessons he had made a mistake. She was now thinking she was so bad at sex it would take a lot longer than she had thought. He wanted to tell her she was great at sex, that he still had flashbacks that left him hard and wanting her. Wanted to yell across the field she was great at sex and whoever told her she wasn't was a moron. Sadly, he knew who that moron was and decided he hated Greg more now than he ever had before. It was a deeper hate now.

Clem was still upset with Ben over whatever happened so Jasper couldn't even use the kids as an excuse to see her. Neither of the kids were talking about what had happened. They didn't even talk as they waited for the bus in the morning.

After about an hour, Evie finally walked onto the field. She had timed it perfectly as Zoey was driving the combine their way. No time for a private conversation.

Private conversation. He smiled, remembering her face as she had explained her favor. Almost immediately he had turned around when she had started talking about dating, he had watched her the entire time. His heart had leaped into his throat. Did she want to date him? But it had dropped when he realized she was talking about dating another man, *any* other man. Then she had started talking about sex and he almost pulled her into his arms, but had resisted because he wanted to hear everything she had to say.

Had she really thought that he would say no to her request? Had she not realized that he could barely keep his hands off her? That he wanted her in his bed and not just for some silly favor. For forever.

By the time Evie had made it to the truck the combine was already there, unloading. Zoey jumped out of the machine and climbed down to the ground, crossing paths with Evie. It was time for her to open the pumpkin patch.

Deciding to intercept Evie before she could climb into the cab of the combine, Jasper rushed to her side and pulled her close to him. Almost shouting so he could be heard over the loud machinery, he said, "You are avoiding me."

Pulling away, he looked into her face and she shook her head. She leaned into him and he felt her breath on his ear before she said, "Don't worry about the favor, forget I ever asked. I don't need help."

He was stunned by her words. What did she mean? He wasn't worried about the favor. It was all he had been thinking about for *days*. There was no way he could forget it now.

Taking advantage of his shock, she pulled away from him and hurried to the combine. Before he knew it, Evie was driving away again. By the time he made it back to the field, Ben had arrived home from school and was ready to help him with the truck. Though it was great to be able to spend time with the boy, he knew the kid was only there so Evie didn't have to talk to Jasper.

"How was school?" Jasper asked.

"Fine," the boy replied.

"Would you rather be over at the pumpkin patch?" Jasper asked, knowing the kids loved spending their evenings over there.

"No, Clem is there. She is just acting weird lately. I don't want to spend time there," Ben admitted.

"Girls can be that way once in a while," Jasper admitted.

"I know, Mom is moody sometimes. I just ignore her when she's like that," Ben stated.

"How is it with just you and your mom?" Jasper asked. He had gotten to spend a lot of time with Ben over the past few weeks. The more he got to know the boy the more impressed he was with how Evie was raising her.

"It's fine, I guess it's all I know. It's always been just us. I like that Zoey came back, and I like Gabe."

"Do you wish your dad was still around?" he asked.

"I don't know. Mom doesn't talk about him, ever. I just wish Mom would find someone like Zoey did. It would be fun to have guys around sometimes," Ben admitted.

"Is your mom looking for someone?" After last night, he knew she wasn't yet.

"No, she never dates or anything. She just works all the time. She is sad a lot, less since Zoey came home though," the boy admitted.

"Do you think dating will make her happy?" Jasper asked.

"It made Zoey happy. I think Mom would be happy too," Ben stated his theory.

"I would like to see your mom happy too. I think we all do." Jasper stopped the truck and Ben jumped out and headed for the combine and his mom.

Watching him walk away Jasper was surprised how much insight the kid had into his mom. He didn't think Evie would be happy with how much her son actually saw.

For the rest of the evening Jasper was unable to get Evie alone with Ben always there. When he finally got the grain truck parked in the shed for the night, she was already walking down her driveway with Ben. With a sigh Jasper wondered if she would be able to avoid him until the fields were bare. In his heart, he knew she could do it. That woman was stubborn.

CHAPTER 11

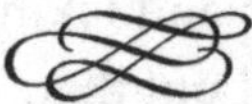

Evie sat at the table drinking coffee and listening to the rain on the windows. She had gotten Ben off to school as usual. Zoey would be staying home today. The younger woman had texted around three a.m. that she was taking a rain day just as the first drops of rain had hit Evie's window. She had been unable to sleep due to the impending rain. Knowing what the rain meant. She had spent most of the night wishing she had never opened her mouth to Jasper.

She had told him that she didn't need his help anymore, but would he listen? Of course he didn't want to have sex with her again, because she had been awful at it the first time. Why would he want to repeat that?

Opening the laptop, she decided that this would be a good day to begin entering her finances into the new program. Waiting for the machine to start up, she was already dreading the process. Maybe she should just go to town and shop for a while.

No, she chided herself, *do your work*. Just because she couldn't get her mind off what might happen didn't mean she still didn't have work to get done. Jasper was probably sitting at home, laughing at her inexperience. Glad she had called it off.

Later she would treat herself to some TV if she got enough data entered into the computer. The computer popped on and she made her way into the program she needed.

She had been working for only a few minutes when the back door opened and slammed shut. She called out to her sister, "I thought you were taking a rain day?"

"I am," said a deeper voice she hadn't wanted to hear, but was dreaming she would. Jasper.

Looking up from the laptop and taking the pencil out of her mouth, she said, "I told you to forget about that."

He walked over to the table, all sexy in jeans and a T-shirt. He must have taken his coat off when he had entered the house along with his shoes or boots, because he made no noise.

He asked, "Do you still want my help?"

"I told you to forget about it," she repeated and tried to keep her eyes on the computer screen. *Ignore him*, she told herself.

"Do you want my help?" he repeated.

"No," she lied and did not look at him, just at the screen.

"Liar," he said, as he slapped the computer shut so she had nothing to look at but him.

Her eyes snapped to his, and she said, "I'm a lost cause, Jasper. Just forget about it."

He looked down at her for a moment and said, "I said I would help you, now I am going to help you. First rain day between Tuesday and Friday, remember?"

She hadn't thought she could get any more nervous than when she had asked him to do this for her, but the panic was tenfold now. She took a deep breath and stood up from the table.

"Okay, fine, let's get this over with," was all she said. Heading for the stairs, she didn't watch if he followed or not.

When she got to the doorway of her bedroom, she realized he had stopped beside her. She heard his footsteps but hadn't dared to check if he was following her or if he had left. Not knowing if she could handle it either way.

"Before we start, how are we going to do this?" she asked, not looking at him.

"What do you mean?" he asked without moving away.

She was having trouble thinking when he was so close.

"Should I take off my clothes or, I don't know, let you take them off?" She stumbled on the words as heat rose to her cheeks. Could he just take a step away?

"I'll take yours off. You have to learn how to take mine off. Does that answer your question?" He took her hands in his and leaned against the door frame. "Any others?"

Biting her bottom lip, she leaned against the opposite side of door frame, so they were looking at each other. Taking a deep breath, she asked, "How many women have you been with? You don't have to answer if you don't want to, it's none of my business."

"Six. Three in college and three since. You?" His body relaxing as he spoke, he was being patient for her.

Evie wondered if she had ever met any of them but couldn't remember him bringing anyone home. But her mind couldn't help but picture them: perfect and young. Or six of them to be exact. She had expected more, way more.

"Just one. Well, two counting you," she admitted, feeling her cheeks heat as she spoke. It sounded normal, perfectly normal, she had been married after all. But if her marriage had been normal she wouldn't be here with Jasper.

Still holding her hands, he lifted them to his mouth and kissed the back of each one. Then he lowered them both back down, just held onto them, as they faced each other in the doorway.

Evie took another deep breath before asking her next question. Not really wanting to know the answer, but unable to stop herself from needing the answer. "How often did you have sex with them?"

"You mean, how often did we have sex or in total?" He was being so nice about the questions.

Closing her eyes, he lifted her hands to his mouth again, she liked when he did that.

She kept her eyes closed as she said, "Either way."

"Maybe two to four times a week, sometimes more, sometimes less. I never really kept track." He was still kissing her hands. "And you, how often for you, Evie?"

Keeping her eyes tightly shut, she didn't want to see the look on his face when she answered, "Just one time."

"A week?" he asked.

"Total," she mumbled, so ashamed of the answer.

He was silent on the other side of her closed eyes. She pulled away from his hands and the doorframe as embarrassment brought unwelcome tears to her eyes. This was exactly what she knew would happen if she ever told anyone. She made it two steps before she felt him grab her from behind in a hug. She sighed with relief, at least he hadn't left.

"You mean that you had sex once and managed to get pregnant that one time?" he asked from behind her, not letting her go.

"Yes," she whispered.

"Why? You were married."

"Greg wanted to wait for marriage when we were in high school."

"And once you were married?" Jasper asked.

"Greg thought I was fat when I was pregnant. Then he said he couldn't look at me while I was nursing, and then he was dead," Evie explained. Still feeling the shame of her husband's words a decade later.

He hugged her closer and said, "God, I hate that man. He was even worse than I had always thought."

"The night he killed himself was the night I left him, that's why Ben and I weren't at the farm when you saw the fire. I was done with him." Only Della and her dad had ever known she had left Greg before he died.

His arms around her made her feel safe, safe enough to tell her deepest secrets. Few people knew some of them and nobody knew them all. It felt right to tell them to Jasper, even if he would be gone in a week.

"Do you think he killed himself because you left him?"

Evie chuckled. "He killed himself because his football career was over. His rushing record had been broken that night. It was all he had left. And he was gay."

"Gay?" Jasper asked.

"Yes, he couldn't accept the fact that he was not attracted to women, he was not attracted to me. Ever," she admitted.

"So Greg wouldn't sleep with you before you got married, or after you got married. How did you get pregnant?" he asked.

She closed her eyes and felt the warm safety of being wrapped in his arms. She leaned her head back against his shoulder and told her most hidden secret, "Greg didn't get me pregnant. I met a guy at a party and things went too far. We had broken up a month before."

Now that it was years later she barely remembered that night, it happened so fast and she had been left more confused than anything. It had been nothing like what had happened in the combine that night was Jasper.

His body stiffened and she tried to pull away, she had made a mistake telling him. She had felt too comfortable with him. It had all been a big mistake.

"Evie, stop." He pulled her back into his arms. "You have just made my day, my year. Not only did that awful man never touch your beautiful body, but Ben has none of his genes. It's like I won the lottery."

"You don't think I am awful? I married a man who didn't love me, who wasn't the father of my baby, and I just let it happen?" Staring out the window across the room she was glad he wasn't looking at her face, because she knew it was awful.

"No, you are amazing. You always have been." He nuzzled her neck. "Why did Greg marry you, when he knew the baby wasn't his?"

"Because he realized he wasn't good enough to play college football. He was flunking out of school. What better way to hide his failure than to return home because he got his girlfriend pregnant? It wasn't really his fault, right? And nobody would guess his secret." With a sigh she admitted, "I went with it because I panicked. I was a stupid kid."

She felt his hands undoing the buttons on her flannel shirt. A small part of her wanted him to stop, that she wasn't ready, but the rest wanted to feel what she had felt in that combine again. She stopped breathing whenever his fingers brushed her bare skin.

"Don't call yourself stupid, things happen," Jasper whispered as he finished the last button.

Evie gasped as his hands cupped her bare breasts. It felt as good as the first time he had held them in his hands. Except this time, she knew it wasn't an accident. He wanted to touch them, to hold them.

His lips left her neck and moved to her ear, then whispered, "Do you ever wear a bra?"

"No," she said on a moan. "I don't need one, they're not that big."

She felt him scrape his nail against her nipple and her knees almost gave out.

"Under the blue dress at the funeral?" he asked.

"No," she said as his hands stopped, slid down her body, and spun her to face him.

"You looked gorgeous in that dress." He lifted her into his arms. "I used to really like that dress, but now I love that dress. I wish I had stripped it off you when I had the chance."

He carried her to the bed, but instead of placing her on it he sat down on the bed and placed her on her feet in front of him. Her shirt was open, and she pulled it closed. Watching him take her hands in his, he kissed the backs of each one and then placed them at her sides. He skimmed his hands up her body and slid the open shirt down her shoulders, letting it fall to the ground in a soft pile.

"Don't hide from me, Evangelina. You're beautiful and I want to see you." As he stared at her breasts for a moment, she resisted the urge to cover her breasts with her hands. He pulled her closer and she felt his lips graze her breast. It felt better than his hands. Without thinking, her hands went into his hair and held his head so he would not leave. As he took more of her breast in his mouth, she arched her back to give him better access, moaning his name as she did.

Despite her hold on his head he moved to her other breast and treated it has he had the first. Evie's knees were starting to buckle under the sensations coursing through her body. Letting go of his black hair, she reached between them and grabbed this front of his T-shirt, trying to pull it from his body. Embarrassment started to set in when the shirt did not move in her hands and his lips left her breasts in the struggle.

"I'm doing this wrong," she whispered, more to herself than to him. They had barely started, and she was failing. Evie bit her bottom lip, trying to stop it from quivering.

Jasper quickly peeled the shirt off his body. Once it was on the floor he stood up, so close that her breasts grazed his chest. Taking her face in his hands he said, "There is no wrong, you are doing everything perfectly."

His lips grazed hers and as she rose to meet his kiss, he took her bottom lip between his and bit down lightly. He deepened the kiss as his tongue touched hers and his fingers dug into her hair. Evie tentatively ran her hands up his strong back, then down it again with more certainty, loving the feeling of his body under her fingers.

Jasper's lips left hers and pulled back less than an inch to say, "I love your hair, I can't even decide if I love it long or short and curly. Either way, I want it free so I can run my fingers through it." Then he kissed her again.

Before she could get her mind around his words, she felt him gently push her down onto the bed. Somehow, he had gotten them turned around without her realizing it. Falling into the middle of the dark purple comforter, for once she didn't think about the fact that she hated the color, but luxuriated in the softness of it on her skin.

With intention she watched him as he unsnapped his pants, then slowly unzip them. She couldn't take her eyes off of his hands or maybe it was what his hands were revealing. Nerves took over and she slammed her eyes shut as he started to push the pants down over his lean hips. But they opened of their own accord to see that he was wearing silky white briefs that left nothing to the imagination.

Her eyes drifted closed once more as he climbed onto the bed beside her. She felt him unsnap and unzip her jeans and then they were gone too. Her eyes were tightly shut as his hand touched her body, running from her thighs, over her belly, skidding over her breast, and to her face and into her hair.

"I can still see you when your eyes are closed," he whispered into her ear, taking the lobe into his hot mouth and sucking on it.

"No, you can't," Her words were stilted as a shot of pure desire went straight from her ear, down her spine, and settled between her legs. Afraid that if she opened her eyes he would see how much she was enjoying this. After all, this wasn't about enjoyment, it was about learning.

"We'll have to stop if you don't open your eyes. You can't learn anything with your eyes closed," Jasper said, his hands leaving her hair and her body.

With everything she had in her she opened her eyes and stared into his brown ones. He was smiling down at her. The way he looked at her made her realize he was right, she needed to see him. His touch might be amazing, but the look he was giving her was ten times hotter.

"Welcome back, there is nothing to be afraid of," he said as he kissed her mouth and then her neck. She started to moan when he took her breast in his mouth again.

Evie gave in to the sensations that were coursing through her body. How he could make her mind completely empty of thought when he touched her, she didn't know. This was even better than their encounter in the combine, however that could be.

She gasped as his hands stroked over her stomach, then lower. As his hands pulled on her panties, skidding them down her hips, she tensed.

He stopped suckling her breast and said, "Trust me."

His lips went back to what they had been doing before and she melted in the mattress because there was no one she trusted more than Jasper. Feeling his hands gently cup her core, she gasped again, but this time with pleasure. As his finger started to move, caressing her core, she moaned, "Jasper."

As she felt the sensations build in her body, she writhed in pleasure as he took her to the peak. She was lost to sensation as the orgasm took hold of her. She knew she was yelling his name, but couldn't stop. "Jas, Jas, Jas," was all she could say.

When her racing heart finally settled down and her mind could process information again, he was lying beside her gently circling her breast with his finger. Then he would lower his head and take the nipple into his mouth and suckle it, then back to circling it all over again.

"Lesson one done," he said grinning at her.

She hadn't been paying attention to the lesson, she had just been letting the sensations engulf her. She had no idea what she had learned, and admitted as much to him. "I didn't do anything."

He continued circling her breast as he said, "You learned to let go, you learned to trust me."

"I did?" she asked. She had not picked up on that.

"You did, next time you won't be as worried."

"Next time?"

She didn't think it would be a good idea for them to have a next time. She didn't even think she could let him go after this time.

He kissed her lips once, twice. "Don't worry about next time. We still have more to enjoy right now." He took her hand in his and placed it on his underwear where his large shaft was nestled.

She would have pulled away but his hand held hers firmly in place. So, she just gave in and started to touch him through the fabric. A groan from him made her feel a little more brave, and she slid her hand under the fabric. He was silkier than she had ever thought, silky and hard. She took him into her hand and started to caress him. In her bravery, she decided she wanted to see him. She let go of his shaft long enough to push his underwear down a little. She took hold of him in her hand again and he slid the material off his body.

Evie enjoyed touching Jasper in this intimate way, but she also loved the way his breath was ragged, and the way she was making him moan. Loving the power it gave her and knowing that he liked her touching him, it didn't matter what she did as long as she was touching him.

She felt his body tense as she stroked him and before she knew what was happening, he had grabbed her hands and flipped her onto her back. His body was lying on hers and he held her hands over her head.

He smiled at her shocked expression and said, "You almost made me explode. I want to be inside you when that happens."

Before she could tell him that was exactly what she wanted, he kissed her and let go of her hands. In her enjoyment of the feeling of his mouth on her body, she just left them above her head and shut her eyes. Relaxing, she let him do what he wanted. There wasn't even a protest when he slid her underwear down and off her body.

Her eyes popped open when she felt his mouth on her core. She would have pulled away but the sensations that had erupted in her body would not allow it. Watching as his mouth moved on her, her head fell back with a moan as his mouth brought her to unimaginable pleasure. "Jas," she cried out.

As the pleasure washed through her body, she felt his mouth leave her, leaving her body pulsing without him. "Jasper, don't stop," she pleaded.

"Never," he said close to her ear. "Never, Evangelina."

Before he finished saying her name, she felt his shaft slowly enter her. The stretch and fullness was even better than his mouth on her had been. Her head fell back again as she moaned, "Jas…per."

When he had filled her to the hilt, he stilled. Her body knew this dance even if her mind did not and started to move. He moaned her name as he joined her rhythm. Then faster and faster, until they both went over the edge together.

CHAPTER 12

JASPER GATHERED Evie into his arms. Hearing the rain softly hitting the window, he knew he would never look at rain the same way again. Just the smell of it would remind him of this woman.

Looking around her bedroom, he saw little of Evie reflected back at him. From the pictures on the walls to the mahogany bedroom set, he thought all the furnishings would look better on display in a museum than in Evie's bedroom. The deep purple comforter and sheets had been a surprise. She was not a purple person. He had hated the material on sight, until he had touched the surprising silky softness. He gently touched the material that would be imprinted on his mind forever: Evie in a purple cloud as he made love to her.

Noticing his perusal, Evie stirred at his side. "It's Della's, her furniture too. She buys stuff and kind of stores it here. The color is awful."

He pulled her closer to him and ran his hand up her naked side. He said, "I will have to thank her one day. I will always remember how you looked as I brought you pleasure on these sheets."

"Oh," was all she said.

Lying with her in his arms he wondered how long it would take for her to stop overthinking her every move. She was worrying about her last action, her last word, and he hated it. Somehow he knew the confident Evie that ran this farm would have the same confidence in the bedroom.

"I hope that you remember it also," he said as he kissed her hair.

"I don't know if the sheets will be the biggest part of that memory," she whispered.

He laughed at her. "Maybe I put the sheets too high on that list myself."

Quiet descended on the room again, as he continued to stroke her skin. They lay on their sides, both facing the window, as the rain tapped against it. He thought that she had fallen asleep until she pulled away from him and grabbed the comforter to cover herself.

"I think this was a mistake." She was looking out the window so he couldn't see her face.

"Why?" he demanded instantly pissed off, he couldn't get a handle on her emotions. Two minutes ago she was content and happy, now she was regretting the entire thing.

"I want to learn the mechanics of sex, Jasper. Instead all I learned was that sex feels good, so good I can't think. If I can't think, I can't learn. I just don't think that I can learn from you. It's too easy to forget that you are just teaching me," she admitted.

He touched her shoulder, the one with the outline of a red heart and said, "That's the way it is supposed to be. If you can think during sex, you're doing it wrong, Evie."

"But I forgot about protection. I forgot to make you use protection," she whispered as her head fell forward.

"Evie," he said gathering her into his arms blanket and all. "I used a condom. You have to realize you weren't there alone. I was with you and I will take care of you."

His hands went around her waist and touched her stomach and as he ruminated on how much he would love to have his baby there. Until this moment he hadn't even thought he wanted kids, but he wanted her to carry his kids.

She shook him off again and got up. "The lesson is over, you can go." She walked naked into the adjoining bathroom and closed the door.

Sitting up in her bed stunned, he realized she had just dismissed him. She went from making love to him to dismissing him in less than twenty minutes. Glancing at the clock he saw it was barely eleven a.m., and the kids were not due home until after three.

Jumping off the bed he grabbed another condom from his pocket and stomped over to the bathroom door. The shower was running when he twisted the knob, and thankfully it was not locked. Quietly he opened the door, slipped in, and shut the door behind him. He walked over to the shower curtain, slipped it open, then stepped into the slippery tub.

"Jasper, what are you doing here?" she said covering her body with her hands.

Closing the curtain behind him, he turned to her. He didn't say a word, just handed her the condom packet. She gingerly took it from him. Sliding his hand into her wet hair he stepped closer to her. They were both under the spray of hot water when his mouth claimed hers in a deep kiss.

"You can be in charge of the protection this time," he said as he lifted her into his arms so he could suckle her wet breasts as the water coursed over them.

He braced her against the wall as he concentrated on her breasts. With gentle movements, he moved her legs, so they were wrapped around him and used one hand to ready her for him. Surprised that she was as ready as he was, he lowered her to her feet and said between clinched teeth, "Put it on. Now."

He watched her shaking hands open the packet and slowly roll the condom over his shaft. There was no way he was helping her. He wanted to see her in control. When it was on, he watched her green eyes widen as he lifted her into his arms again and her legs went around him automatically. He slowly lowered her onto his shaft as she purred his name, then match his movements with the same frenzy. Their orgasms came quickly in the hot, wet shower.

When the water turned cold, Jasper reached over and shut it off. Not letting Evie away from the shower wall, he had pinned her to, he said, "Lessons are not done until I say they are."

At his words her mouth opened to argue, then snapped closed again. It seemed even Evie didn't have anything against his statement.

Moving away from the wall but still keeping her in his arms, he pulled the shower curtain back. Stepping out of the tub, he grabbed a towel from the rack on the way out of the room. He wrapped it around her as they moved across the room.

When he finally let her go, he dropped her onto the bed, then crawled in after her. To his relief she laughed when she landed on the bed. He was worried that he had scared her with his passion. Now he knew she had enjoyed it. He took her face in his hands so he could look into her gorgeous green eyes as he said, "I have to teach you to turn off those voices in your head."

As he thought it might, the laughter left her eyes at the words. He could feel her pull away from him without even moving. "If you just talk to me about it, I can help you."

"I know you are only here because I asked you to. You don't really want to be with me. Like this." She shut her eyes.

He now knew it was a defensive action.

"If I didn't want to be here with you, I wouldn't be here with you. I've wanted to be here since I watched you braid that gorgeous hair in front of me. You turned me on just running your hands through your hair," he said to her and watched as a blush started at her breasts and moved up to her face.

"I didn't know," she whispered.

"I know, that made it even hotter." He touched her hair, now wet and wavy. "I can't believe you cut it off."

"It was in the way." Her eyes were glued to his.

"I loved when it fell on my lap during the funeral. I just wanted to touch it." He sifted his fingers through the golden strands that had so captivated him that day.

"See, in the way," she pointed out.

"When I made love to you in the combine, it was everywhere. In my hands, spilling all over my body, making a curtain around our bodies as I entered you." His hands had stopped moving, all he was doing was staring into her eyes, watching her mind spin with the information.

"I'm sorry I cut it," she whispered.

"I love the way it curls now. It begs me to touch it. You don't braid it every day so I can imagine myself running my hands through it now," he said as her breath caught.

He kissed her lips, then said, "Now I will tell you that I love that my name is too long for you to say when we make love. I love when you call me Jas, because my touch is so good you can't manage two syllables."

He loved that her breath caught at the words. He was going to enjoy the rest of the day and he was determined that she would too.

* * *

EVIE WATCHED Jasper walk down the driveway as the bus pulled up to drop off the kids. She wished he would have stayed for supper, but with the kids fighting that was would be hard to sell to Clem and Ben.

Ben greeted Jasper as they passed each other on the driveway. Hopefully, her son would not suspect something had happened between his mom and their neighbor.

Jasper was supposed to have left a half an hour before Ben's bus came, but neither could stop kissing each other until Jasper had seen the bus in the distance. Only then had she been able to get him out the door.

She smiled at the memory of the rain day. She had never spent a full day naked before, but Jasper had insisted no clothes were needed, even for lunch. This morning she would never have thought she would ever feel comfortable standing naked in her kitchen with a naked man. But she had, and it was great.

Her son entered the house with little greeting for his mother, and she went to the kitchen to get him something to eat. She didn't press the boy on what was going on with him and Clem, because it wasn't her business. Though she hoped the rift wouldn't last very long.

"How was your day?" she asked, cautiously.

"Fine," came the one-word answer.

"Did you do anything fun?"

"No. I'm going to my room." He left her alone in the kitchen.

Should she worry about her son? Zoey's image as a teenager sped through her mind. From the age of sixteen until eighteen Zoey had been in more trouble than anyone Evie had ever known. She had snuck out, broken car windows, got kicked out of school, and started a fire in the high school. She denied starting the fire to this day, but she had admitted to breaking into the building that night.

Evie sat at the table and wondered if she should talk to her sister about Ben. Not that he had ever gotten into trouble, but was he heading in that direction? It seemed now that Zoey was back home reminding Evie of the past, it was making her more nervous about her son. She didn't know how she would handle an out-of-control boy. She had been no help with an out-of-control sister.

Still disappointed in herself with how much she had missed back then, Evie tried to remind herself that she had a lot on her mind then. Maybe if she had not been so wrapped up in her own stuff, she would have seen Zoey needed help.

Was she getting too wrapped up in Jasper that she was missing things about her own son? Was she not paying enough attention, and that was why he was so moody?

The questions swirled around in her head when the phone rang. It was Jasper, just seeing his name made her smile. Picking up her cell-phone, she asked, "Is yours as mad as mine?"

He sighed into the phone. "Yup, she is not talking to me."

"Mine either," she admitted.

"I guess I can't come over to see you again today," he said.

"No, I guess not. See you tomorrow, Jasper," she said into the phone, wishing she was saying it to his face.

"Good night, Evie. I'll miss you." And he hung up the phone.

She sighed and put the phone back on the table, she would miss him too. More than she ever thought she would.

CHAPTER 13

Jasper was out of bed early the next morning, ready to get this day going. Rain or shine he would get to see Evie again. He had hoped for rain, so when the sun rose bright and clear, he was a little disappointed.

Sitting on the porch he watched the two kids at the end of the driveway waiting for the bus. The tension between them could be seen even from where he sat. They were still at odds this morning. The big yellow bus came and went, taking their preteen drama with it.

He was still sitting on the porch when he saw the two women leave the house across the road. No matter what, Zoey always went to Evie's first, then they came over to his grandmother's fields. Evie never came over without her sister, if Zoey was scheduled to help that day. As they walked, he could tell they were in conversation. Both had a habit of talking with their hands, Zoey more than Evie, but Evie was guilty of it also.

As they approached, he saw that Evie was wearing a light raincoat over her blue flannel shirt and jeans. He now knew she wouldn't be wearing a bra, and it made his hands itch thinking of them free from confines. He got up to meet them on the road.

"Morning," he said to them both, but with his gaze only on Evie. She was all he had eyes for.

"Morning, Jasper," she responded.

"Morning," Zoey said, not noticing she was not actually a part of the conversation.

"It will be too wet today for anything. But I thought I would look over the equipment. The combine was making a noise that I should look at. I would have come over yesterday but I just took a day for me." Evie's cheeks were scarlet as she added the last for Zoey he assumed.

Jasper knew exactly what she had been up to all day.

"Well, you need a day for you," Zoey said.

"Did you enjoy your day off?" Jasper asked with a smile, loving the pink in her cheeks. When she was not avoiding him, she was a lot of fun.

"Yes, I did enjoy it," Evie mumbled as they entered the shed.

Jasper turned on the light and Evie went over to the combine and started to open doors he never knew were there. Zoey sat down on one of the four chairs in the shed and patted the one next to her.

"She doesn't need either of us. But you have to be ready—she will yell for a wrench or something and you have to bring it to her." Zoey had obviously done this many times before.

"I'll sit here then." He sat down and watched for glimpses of Evie's body as she worked.

"What did you do yesterday?" Zoey asked.

"I did a favor for a friend," he said innocently.

BANG!

A loud noise clanged from Evie's direction and Jasper smiled at her reaction.

"Are you okay, Evie?" Zoey asked.

"Yes, I'm fine, just fine," Evie yelled.

"Is Gabe back at work?" he asked Zoey.

"No, he's off until Saturday. Which stinks, because I have to do the pumpkin patch and Evie has to do the farmer's market. I could really use his help," Zoey explained.

"Is Della coming home to help?" he asked.

"No, she is looking for a job. She needs to concentrate on that and not on selling my pumpkins," Zoey explained.

"I can help," he offered. So far he hadn't helped at all at the pumpkin patch. With all the combining, he hadn't even had time to wander over there in the daylight.

"Oh I was planning on it. You'll be with me and Evie will take the kids with her to the market." Zoey winked.

"The kids are fighting," he told her, realizing Evie must not have told her about their feud.

"About what?"

"We don't know, neither of us has been able to get anything out of them. It's been a few days now."

He caught a glimpse of Evie before she vanished again.

"Did you ask them?" Zoey asked.

"No." He hadn't thought to just ask the kids what had happened.

"Maybe they will tell you, maybe they won't. Kids," Zoey said, like she had raised dozens of them.

At that point, Evie asked for a tool, but before he could get up, Zoey hopped to her feet and grabbed it and brought it to the hidden woman.

"Then I guess we shouldn't send them with Evie alone. They will make her life miserable," Zoey said when she got back to her chair.

"It will," he agreed. When Evie called for another tool, he glanced at Zoey, but she didn't get up. Apparently, it was his turn. He got up, grabbed the tool, and headed to the back of the shed.

He found Evie working on something that her body blocked from his view. He walked up behind her and whispered in her ear as he wrapped his arm around her waist, "I have your wrench, beautiful." He felt her body lean back into his as he held her.

"Thanks," she whispered back.

He spun her in his arms and lightly kissed her smiling mouth. Lifting his head, he kissed her nose and handed her the tool and she turned back to her work. Walking back out to sit by Zoey, he waited for his next turn to deliver a tool with excitement.

He decided that Zoey hadn't noticed a thing when she asked, "Do you think the kids would be okay at the farm all day? They wouldn't have to be close to each other."

"I think that would be okay." Jasper tried to sound calm, but all he could think about was two days alone with Evie, with just a farmers Market to occupy their time.

"Then you can go with Evie to Minneapolis. I will keep both the kids. It will be busy, but I think we can handle it," Zoey decided.

"What are you guys planning out here?" Evie asked as she came out carrying the wrench Jasper had brought her.

"You and Jasper are going to Minneapolis for the market on Saturday," Zoey told her sister with a smile.

"He doesn't have to," Evie instantly protested.

"Yes, he does, you can't do it alone. Not during pumpkin season. You need a strong young man to lift them for you. I volunteered Jasper," Zoey said, leaning over and feeling his arm for muscles. "I am removing the strong part. Just an able body for you, Evie."

Evie blushed and Jasper wondered what had just gone through her mind. "I am strong enough to lift a pumpkin or two, maybe even more than a pumpkin."

Zoey laughed and said, "I doubt that. You have always been a weakling and now you just have that office job."

"I think I will be just fine, Zoey," he said, trying not to laugh.

Zoey jumped to her feet. "Jasper, don't you have a place downtown?"

"Yes, why?"

"You and Evie can stay there instead of Della's. Then you won't have that forty-five minute drive in the morning. Evie can sleep on your couch, unless you have a spare room," Zoey said, pacing a little.

"That could work," Jasper said with an excitement he could barely hide from the redhead.

Evie jumped in, "No, I cannot impose. I can stay at Della's."

"Then you have to add a stop to pick up Jasper that morning and also drop him off on Friday. That's too much work. You can sleep on his couch." Zoey had it all planned out.

"What about the kids, who is going to watch them?" Evie asked.

"I will, Gabe and I. They can go to their own rooms at my place and ignore each other. They will be fine," Zoey said.

Jasper looked at the sisters and asked, "What time would we have to leave tomorrow?"

Why was she trying to get out of going with him to Minneapolis? He had to get the plan finalized before she actually came up with a real reason to not go.

"You guys should quit when I do, no reason to keep working when you have a drive in front of you," Zoey said.

Jasper wondered if Zoey was trying to push them together or had no idea what was happening beneath her nose. All he knew was that he was just going let it happen, it was working out great for him.

Evie would not look at Jasper. "I guess that could work."

"Are you done?" Zoey asked, referring to the combine.

"No," Evie said. "But I need a part in town. I will run and get it."

"No, I can," Zoey said.

"No, you go home and be with Gabe. He is off work today, and I don't want the details," she said to her sister, then turned to Jasper. "You can go too. I can handle this."

Zoey was off her chair, had hugged her sister, and was heading out the door with a backwards goodbye almost before Evie had finished. Neither noticed her leave because they couldn't take their eyes off each other.

"Good morning, Evie," Jasper said with a smile.

"Good morning, Jasper." She smiled back at him not hiding it anymore.

"Is it another rain day?" He took a step toward her.

"No, I really have to get that part. Sorry." She bit her lip.

"Nothing to be sorry about, you have to work. Do you want a ride to town?" He took another step toward her.

"No, I can do it. But maybe once its fixed I can come find you. If you want?" She didn't move, but didn't shy away either.

"Can't I help you with it? Might get it done faster. And you won't have to come find me." He took another step closer so that they were touching.

"I don't need help," she protested.

"Can I help you anyway?" he said as he nuzzled her neck.

"I can handle it." Despite her assurances, she leaned her head so he had better access to her neck.

"I know you can, but I want to help."

He grabbed her hands, about to kiss her when her phone pinged an alert. He watched as she took it out of her coat pocket and read the long text. With his now free hand, he reached out to touch her hair.

She pulled away from him as another text sounded.

"What is it?" he asked, realizing it must be something important as two more notifications in a row came and she pulled away, silently reading.

"Evie, what is it?" He was getting nervous it was something serious. Was it one of the kids?

When she finally looked up, she had tears in her eyes, but then she launched herself into his arms and hugged him tight. He only stopped worrying it was bad news when he heard her say into his chest, "Della's moving back. I'm going to have both my sisters back."

With that he lifted her as he hugged her back and spun her around. He was about to kiss her happy lips when the shed door flung open. At the sight of her sister, Evie was out of his arms in an instant and had run across the shed, throwing her arms around Zoey. Jasper watched the sisters hugging and laughing.

Della was only moving two hours north, and they saw her often as it was. But he knew some of the sisters' emotions came from when Zoey was in the Army and never came home. This excitement had more to do with those uncertain times than it did with Della coming home. Though both sisters would love having another close by.

"Are you taking Jasper?" he heard Zoey saying. Suppressing a laugh, he thought that had been the plan before the text had come in.

"He doesn't want to go," Evie said, without even asking him.

"Maybe he does," he said and hugged the two women still holding onto each other. Maybe it was an excuse to touch Evie again. "Where are we going?"

Evie pulled away. "Della is going to move into the mansion so we have to go see what needs to be done before that can happen."

"Sounds fun. I'm in," he said. He wasn't missing a moment he could spend with Evie, he would be leaving soon. But he didn't want to think about that now.

"Let's meet there," Zoey said. "I will go get Gabe and you guys can ride together."

"Why don't we ride together and Gabe can meet us there?" Evie argued.

Suddenly he saw that she was nervous to be alone with him. What had happened over night that had caused that?

"Because you'll make us stop to get that part you need for the combine first. I want to skip the tractor store part of the trip. Boring. I want to get to the fun part. And I want to tell Gabe the good news in person," Zoey said and walked out the door without letting Evie say another word.

"I have to go home," Evie said. She was clearly getting more nervous around him every moment. She was getting jumpy.

"I can drive," he didn't like her sudden distance.

"I need to get the key for the house." She started to leave.

Before she could take a step he grabbed her by the arm pulling her back to him. Knowing she was pushing him away, he wanted to remind her of the day before and all that had happened between them. Drawing her completely into his arms, he finally kissed her soft lips. As he deepened the kiss he could feel her body melted into his, feel the tension release from her body.

Breaking the kiss, he said, "Evie, it's just me, okay? No need to be nervous. I know you're overthinking what we did yesterday, but you don't have to. I want to spend time with you." He lightly kissed her again and taking her hand in his, they started for the door.

They ended up taking her truck, anyway. She didn't want to get grease in his car. Jasper laughed when he realized that Zoey was right. Evie had wanted to stop at the tractor store to get what she needed before arriving at the old house.

Getting out of the pickup in front of Birch Cove's haunted mansion, Jasper looked up at the building badly in need of new paint and shingles. When he had been in high school, the big thing had been to dare someone to go into the house. He had never had the balls to do it. He knew Zoey had taken the dare and had spent over ten minutes in the house. Now that he knew her family owned the house, maybe his friend hadn't been as brave as he had thought she was at the time.

"The porch needs work," Evie commented as she walked up them onto the huge porch. "There used to be a swing over there. I guess someone stole it. When we were little Della and I used to play on the porch the most, I don't know why, but we always played outside. Zoey wasn't born yet."

Watching as she pulled out the key and opened the door, Jasper jumped a little when the door squeaked like a proper haunted house. Putting the key back in her pocket, she took his hand in hers and said, "I will protect you from the ghosts."

"Thanks," he said sarcastically, but pulled her hand to his lips and kissed it.

Walking into the house, it was nothing like he expected. The ceilings were high and the woodwork was gorgeous, where it wasn't painted. There wasn't a piece of furniture in the place as far as Jasper could see and the dust was deep. Footprints dotted the ground from where the sisters had visited over the weekend.

"I thought Zoey would beat us here, we even had a stop to make," Jasper said.

"They probably got distracted. It happens with them," Evie said.

"That's what you want, to be distracted?" Jasper asked, remembering that she had said she wanted to have what Zoey had with Gabe.

"Something like that," Evie said sounding distracted, but was it the house that was distracting her?

Slowly they wandered through the rooms on the main floor. Most were in better shape than Jasper would have expected for a house that had been empty most of his life. There were bold colors on almost every wall, none of which actually matched the others. The entryway and the adjoining living room had not been to damaged, but a careless painter had dribbled orange paint all over the vintage woodwork in the dining room and the office. The floors were carpeted but had seen better days while the kitchen in the back of the house was almost unusable as the cabinets were falling from the walls. The grand staircase had been left alone, but there were pieces that needed replacing. Jasper didn't know how long it would take to get this place in order, but months seemed like a generous time frame.

They were still holding hands as they went up the wide staircase. Jasper had never seen a more elaborate staircase in his life. The carvings on it were beautiful. Again, he wondered how anyone could have abandoned this house for all those years.

"Why doesn't anyone live here?" He pointed at the cobwebs hanging from the ceiling laden with dust.

"Dad rented it for a few years and the renters painted. He said never again. Since Grandpa and Grandma wanted us girls to have it, he kept it empty," Evie said as she lead them up the staircase.

The upstairs was in a lot better shape than the downstairs. A good cleaning, new carpet, and paint and it would be livable up here. The bathrooms were serviceable, but would probably need to be redone in time.

They walked into the master bedroom that contained a huge fireplace that dominated the space. Evie tugged away and drifted over to the massive fireplace, dragging a finger through the dust on top of the mantel.

"There was a four-poster bed in this room, it was huge and old. I brought it home but it never fit in my house. It's in the garage out back. I suppose there isn't much furniture left now," she said and wandered over to inspect the closet.

When she walked past Jasper, he pulled her into his arms, needing to feel her warmth. He was surprised when she kissed him first, but not surprised enough to not kiss her back. Placing his hands on her butt he pulled her closer to him.

She pulled out of his arms when a door on the floor below slammed shut. Watching her try to catch her breath like a guilty teenager made him laugh. Fighting the urge to pull her back into his arms for another kiss was hard. He took her hand as Zoey called her name from downstairs.

"Act natural," he whispered as they got to the stairs. He had intended to drop her hand at the stairs but continued holding it, unable to break the contact just yet. But he instantly dropped it when Zoey spoke.

"Stop!" Zoey yelled, looking right at Jasper and Evie. "Jasper, come down here."

He walked slowly down the stairs, wondering what Zoey would say about his holding Evie's hand. He had no idea what Evie's sisters would think of them as a couple. But he was ready to battle Evie's redheaded sister over the woman he was in love with.

Zoey dismissed him as she said, "Thanks, Jasper. Now, Evie, come down slowly. See, Gabe? See how beautiful it will be?"

"I just said it was pretty dirty," Gabe insisted.

"What's going on?" Evie asked as she descended the staircase.

Zoey spun in a circle at the bottom of the stairs and said to them all, "This is where I am getting married."

As Jasper watched Evie walk down the stairs, he became fully caught up in Zoey's vision. Only instead of picturing Zoey in a wedding dress descending the stairway, Jasper saw Evie in white. It had taken his breath away.

"We only have three months before you get married, Zoey, unless you move back the date. There's too much to do to get the house ready in that short amount of time." As usual, Evie was the voice of reason.

"No way, the date stays. We have a lot to do before then—but we have to clean it anyway for Della. We can totally have my wedding here. I can see it. Can't you see it too? For me, guys?" Zoey pleaded with them, her eyes full of hope like a little child.

Evie got to the bottom of the stairs and sighed. "You will have to talk to Della, it's her house."

After a quick phone call, Della was convinced and the wedding was set. Zoey was ready to get started right that moment. Gabe and Jasper spent the rest of the day ripping out carpets and cleaning walls and floors. To Jasper's frustration, Evie left by midday to fix the combine, alone, as Jasper hadn't figured out a good excuse to go with her.

Soon after Evie left, Jasper called a buddy from high school who did carpentry locally. Within an hour, Chad Monroe swung by to check out the place. To Zoey's delight, the carpenter agreed to get started immediately, his only request was that he didn't want work to conflict with his weekend band gigs. After a quick call to an oddly agreeable

Della, he was hired to do as much work refinishing the woodwork as possible before Christmas.

Still upset with Evie, Jasper couldn't help but catch the excitement from the group. Even Chad had agreed to start that day so that as much work as possible could get done before the holiday wedding. A wedding Zoey couldn't stop talking about all day.

When Gabe and Jasper had removed the carpets, they had revealed the original hardwood floors throughout the house. As each new detail was revealed, Jasper decided it would be a beautiful place to get married, and a great place for a law firm. He could see the potential.

By the time Gabe and Zoey dropped him off, the kids were just getting off the bus. Each kid headed for their house without a word to each other, it seemed the fight was still on. Back at his grandma's house he checked the shed first, since Clem wasn't exactly talking to him either. Evie, it seemed, was done with the combine and had gone home, because the shed was empty.

With the kids still not talking he had no excuse to go see Evie, so he went into the house to take a shower and feed his cousin. Maybe Clem was ready to talk to him about what was going on.

CHAPTER 14

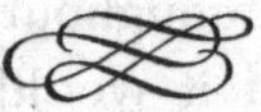

Pulling on her jacket, Evie slipped out of the house into the brisk night air. It was close to ten p.m. and Ben had been sleeping for almost an hour. Lecturing herself as she headed down the driveway that he would be fine on his own, she reminded herself that he was eleven for heaven's sake and soundly sleeping.

Her footsteps slowed as she got closer to Grandma Betty's house— the house where Jasper was staying. Sitting down on the front porch, she wondered if he actually wanted to see her. This afternoon she had abandoned him with Zoey and Gabe, but he was used to spending time with the couple, at least he usually spent more time with them than her in the afternoons.

Pulling her phone out of her pocket, she sent him a text.

Evie: Meet me on the porch.

Then she waited nervously in the chilly night. The full moon above gave everything in the yard an eerie glow. After a few minutes, she got up and headed back home, disappointed. She had been wrong. She had thought he might want to see her. Another thing she was wrong about.

By the time her shoes hit the gravel of the driveway she just wanted to run. Get away from here as soon as possible. How had she thought that she could do a relationship? Even if whatever they were doing wasn't an actual relationship.

Had she not told him she was no good at this? But she had pushed forward anyway. Mistake. She was always making mistakes. Could she get anything right in this life?

Letting the tears flow, she walked away from Jasper, toward her house, toward her bed. Crawling into bed and pulling the covers over her head was her only goal now.

It seemed colder now than when she had first stepped outside, giddy with nerves. Cold was seeping into her entire body. Would she ever warm back up?

When she got to the county road, she paused and almost turned back. Instead, she stuffed her hands deeper into her coat pockets and went on.

"Evie?" Jasper called into the dark behind her.

Heart in her throat, she spun around and breathed, "Jasper, you scared me."

"Where are you going?" he asked, she could see he was smiling in the dim light.

"Home. You didn't come out."

"Sorry, I just got your message. But you were already running home."

"I decided I made a mistake," she said, wiping her tears from her face with her coat sleeve.

"What mistake?"

"Coming over here, thinking you wanted to see me." She forced the tears back.

"I want to see you all the time. I want to be with you all the time." He took her hands into his. "What do you want to do now that you have me out of the house?"

What did he mean by his declaration? Wasn't this all a part of the favor? Wasn't this all about sex for him? Dismissing them as just word she cleared her throat and said, "I thought we could go for a walk. Talk."

Dropping one of her hands, he pulled her to start walking down the road. "I can walk and talk with you, Evie."

Silently they strolled down the road hand in hand. As they went, Jasper pulled her hand up to his mouth and kissed it. "How was your day, Evie?"

"Good. I got the combine fixed, so it is ready for tomorrow. Ben was still in a bad mood. How was the housecleaning?"

"Thank you for leaving me behind to help with that. I can't believe how dirty that carpet was," he said, but the smile in his eyes let her know he didn't mind.

"Sorry, I should have taken you with me. But they needed your help more than I did," she admitted.

"I didn't mind helping, maybe next time just ask? Don't make all the decisions for me," he said.

"I have a bad habit of making decisions for everyone. Just ask Zoey. I am working on it, but it is a hard habit to break," she said.

"It is something I noticed about you. You have to give up some control to those around you."

His hand was warm in hers.

"I am trying. I just spent too many years making all the decisions without anyone's help or even input. It was all on me to decide when and how things got done. I know the best way to do things after a lot of trial and error and have a hard time letting others make the mistakes I've already made. I'm good at knowing where people are needed the most." Evie tried to convey how hard it was to make all the decisions for herself and her young son after her husband and father died as they walked.

"No one doubts your experience. But you might get more cooperation if you let everyone have a say," he said.

"I really have been trying. I almost lost Zoey again this spring because I had a hard time listening to her. Since then I have really been working on it," Evie said.

"What happened with Zoey?" he asked.

"She'd only been home from the Army a few weeks but I wasn't doing a very good job of treating her like my sister instead of a farm-hand. She got so fed up and we said things we shouldn't have. Or I did. I think she was ready to leave." Evie leaned into his body as they walked.

"I can't see you having a big enough fight for her to leave, you two fight all the time," Jasper told her with a smile.

"I said some things that weren't very kind, things that were better left unsaid." Evie hated thinking about that day, the tears and the pain.

"What did you say?" he asked as their footsteps slowed.

"I said she wouldn't stay at the farm for long, that she would find something else she wanted to do before fall. Then she said she had always wanted to be here, to farm, but since coming back nothing she did was good enough for me," Evie confessed into the night.

"And?" he questioned.

"And she said that she and Dad did not get along in the end because he was not her father. She said he had raised her because he couldn't find our mom." She bit her lip against the pain of the memory of the hurt in Zoey's eyes when she had yelled the words at her.

"Do you believe her?" Jasper wanted to know.

"Yes and no. No, mainly because I don't *want* to believe it. And yes, because I saw how Dad treated Zoey during high school. Like he was tired of her and ready to be done. Parenting is not like that. You never get to be done. You never want to be done," she said.

"Do you still think that she is looking for something better?"

"No, she loves the farm as much as I do. I can see that now. Back then I can say I really didn't know my baby sister. It had been years since I had lived with her, or even spent much time with her. That's when I started to make a point to show her, and Della, how much I care about them all the time. We are sisters and need to be closer than we were," she admitted.

No longer was she standoffish with them, hugs were frequent now as were words of encouragement and love.

"How about you? Do you love it?" Jasper asked.

"Farming? Yes, I love it. Since I started at the farmer's markets, it has gotten better and better. The grain farming is okay, but I do it so that I can sell my vegetables at the farmer's markets," she admitted her secret. She had just spent days harvesting corn with him and she didn't enjoy it as much as picking weeds.

"What do you really think of Zoey and Gabe as a couple?"

"Why do you ask?"

"Because Grandma said you were not happy when they started dating. Has that changed or not?"

"You're right, I wasn't happy. I couldn't see that they are perfect for each other, all I could see was the differences. I worry sometimes that it won't last, that the fire will burn out. It all happened so quickly. They are getting married so quickly. They haven't even known each other long. I don't want to see her hurt. When they broke up last spring, she was shattered. It lasted for nearly a month and I never want to see her like that again."

"But you are envious of their relationship?" Their steps were still slow as he asked.

"Yes. They are so in love, sometimes it hurts to look at them. They only see each other—nobody else exists. I want someone to look at me like that one day," she whispered the last words.

Jasper pulled her to a stop in the road and pulled her into his arms for a hug. Melting into his warm body, she sighed. Evie realized that she didn't want somebody to look at her like that, she wanted Jasper to look at her like that. The realization scared her and she pulled out of his arms, away from his comfort. Needing space, but not too much ,she took his hand and started back the way they came.

"What do *you* think of Zoey and Gabe as a couple?" she asked him the same question, curious about his opinion as an outsider.

"I have to admit that it is sometimes uncomfortable. All the looks and the touching if they get too close to one another. I mean Zoey deserves it, she deserves to be everything to him," he said.

"She does deserve it," Evie said quietly.

"You deserve it, too. Everybody deserves to be loved like that." Again, he raised the hand that he was holding and kissed the back of it.

His words warmed her in the chilly night. For some reason coming from him, she could almost believe him. Almost. Once he was gone she was going back to her old way, no men for her. No other man could be as good as this man right here.

"I think he lets her win when they fight," Jasper mused.

"Oh, she can hold her own in an argument."

He laughed. "I know she can, but today she flipped him like she likes to do with me, and he let it happen. There he was on the ground in a pile of dirty carpets staring up at her like she walked on water. I know he could have stopped the flip from happening, but he didn't. I wonder if he didn't want it to happen."

"They are always doing that. Showing off their defensive training. He is always letting her win. It's how he is," Evie admitted. "Now I know that he is the best thing that happened to Zoey. I don't know if she would have come out her depression if not for him. Well, she would have, but it would have taken a lot longer."

"He is good for her and good to her," he said pulling her to him as they walked the last few yards to the end of their joined driveways.

"This is where we part," Evie said.

"I wish I could drag you home with me, or you could drag me home with you. I want to be with you," he said as he pulled her into his arms.

"Me too," she whispered as his mouth touched hers lightly in the dark.

Letting him deepen the kiss she slid her hand under his coat so she could feel his body heat. His hands slid in her hair, holding her in place as his mouth took its fill of her.

Slipping away from his arms and taking a step back, Evie said, "I will see you tomorrow, Jasper."

In the dim light, she saw him smile. "Tomorrow I get to have you in my bed, Evie. All night."

"That's the only reason I can walk away tonight," she admitted.

"Good night, Evie." He touched her cheek.

"Good night, Jasper." She took another step away from him.

Both just stood there, looking at each other, three feet apart. Neither moved to leave, neither moved to get closer. Both just stared into each other's eyes in the semidarkness.

"Tomorrow," Jasper said.

Evie's mind immediately jumped to images of what it would be like when they were alone together once again tomorrow. The images were so vivid she felt her cheeks getting hot. Embarrassed, she spun around and briskly walked toward her house. She did not turn to see if he was following, going to his house, or just standing watching her go.

It didn't matter what he was doing right now, tomorrow at this time she would be in his arms. Tomorrow.

CHAPTER 15

EVIE WATCHED the sunset from the driver's seat of her pickup. The farmer's market had been a success, and it was great to have help lifting all the heavy pumpkins from a strong adult. Glancing over at the man who was looking at his phone, he must have felt her gaze because he glanced up and smiled at her. His smile was gorgeous.

Smiling back at him, she couldn't believe how happy she was. The last two days had been amazing. He had been amazing.

After saying goodbye to the two kids at Zoey and Gabe's, they made it to his apartment around six that night due to heavy traffic. They hadn't had supper until close to ten, and she had not slept on the couch. Happily, she had spent the night in his arms in his warm bed. This time she hadn't had the nervousness of the first time, she just enjoyed being with him.

Jasper had set the alarm for an hour earlier than they needed. The explanation he gave was that he wanted to wake her up properly. And he had succeeded, in her mind. It was the way she wanted to wake up every morning for the rest of her life.

When they had finally gotten to the farmer's market they had arrived later than she usually liked to get there. They had to work fast to get the tables set up and the vegetables out to beat the early morning crowd. Evie was extra grateful for Jasper's help moving the truckload of pumpkins to the grass around her booth so that customers could wander and pick out the ones they liked. Luckily she had brought a lot, because they spent the rest of the day constantly replenishing their stock.

The day had been spent holding hands and acting like teenagers in love in the midst of a sea of strangers. Jasper stole kisses or made jokes while Evie made change until she couldn't help but laugh. It was nice to be able to not have to be on guard with him. She loved having him around, it had made everything easier and fun.

After their relaxed and enjoyable day, she wished that they were in a real relationship. That today was like every other day and they didn't have to hide it from the people they love. She wanted to be able to kiss and touch him even when her sisters or Ben were around. But of course, she wanted him forever also.

As she drove home, he took her hand from the steering wheel and pulled it to his lips to kiss it. She had gotten used to him kissing her, even her hand, but it still sent a bolt of electricity down her spine every time. It still thrilled her.

"Are you excited to get home?" he asked.

"Yes and no, I love spending time with you alone, but I miss Ben and hated leaving the corn standing when I should be combining it." She tore her eyes from his and looked back out the windshield. Remembering that once the corn was gone, so was Jasper.

"How long do you think we have left?" he asked.

"Three days, maybe less," she admitted. The time was growing short for their relationship.

"What happens then?" he asked.

Evie knew he was talking about them she wasn't ready to talk about that, not after the last two days of being with him every minute of the day. Her mind wasn't ready.

"Then I start cultivating and you go back to that great apartment and to work." She hated the words even as she said them. Their time together was coming to an end.

"What about us?" he asked as Birch Cove came into view.

Pulling her hand away, she pretended that she needed two hands to steer. She couldn't touch him during this conversation. This was the conversation she had been dreading since they had made love the first time. She never wanted to say any of these words.

"There is no us, Jasper. It was just a favor."

She was not able to look at him. No way could she look into those brown eyes and say what had to be said. He would leave and she had wanted to start dating, but she couldn't even plan that while he was still there. She just hoped she could when he was gone.

"Is that still what you think happened between us, a favor?" he demanded.

Her inner voice was screaming no, but her outer voice said, "Yes."

"Liar," he bit out. "You have worn that bastard's ring for a dozen years, but you won't even try with me. I am nothing like him."

"I know," she glanced at the ring still on her finger. Trying to take it off had failed miserably. They were almost home but Evie didn't know if she make it there without him seeing her cry.

"Why do you wear his ring still? I know you don't love him and that you never did, so why the ring?" His voice was demanding.

"I don't ever think of him when I look at it. We only used it as a wedding ring because Greg was too drunk to remember he needed one," she admitted, looking at the gold band.

"Do you wear it to warn off men? Because I know the truth and it does not work with me," he said.

"No." Shaking her head, she pulled into his yard.

Why did he have to push her now? Why not wait until the end and just walk away? Like he was supposed to.

"Then why, Evie?" he demanded.

"I wear it because it reminds me of all the things I will never have. Goodbye, Jasper."

She knew he deserved a better explanation. But she couldn't do it today, not now. She was not going to hold back the tears much longer.

Turning to look out the driver side window, Evie hid her face so she wouldn't have to watch him walk away. Didn't have to watch him leave her. Hearing him grab his bag from the back seat and slam the door made the tears start to flow. She had to get away before she fell apart completely. Pulling away from his house, she drove across the road to her own. She sat in the car for a long time, letting the tears flow, knowing Ben would be over at Zoey's helping with the pumpkin patch. Nobody was here to watch her, question her every move. See her cry.

Lifting her hand, she looked at the ring there. She knew she had to take it off. The last time Jasper had said something about it she had tried. But it represented the kind of love she longed for and had never been able to find. At least until she had let herself fall for Jasper. Taking off the ring, she held it in her palm. Maybe she was afraid that if she took off the ring, she would be admitting that she would forget that the kind of love she wanted was out there. That she would never find that perfect kind of love it represented without the ring there to remind her.

But now looking at the gold band, she knew that kind of love existed, with or without the ring. It was the love she felt for Jasper. But Jasper didn't feel that for her, and in three days he would go back to his life and forget about her completely. She would remain here, without him, still in love with him.

Opening the pickup door, she slipped the gold band into the pocket of her jeans. Maybe she should just give it to Gabe for Zoey. They were getting married at the Connor Mansion. Maybe he would like to give her the Connor ring. The ring would then be a part of another great love story. One that it would never be a part of her.

Grabbing her bag from the back seat, she went into her house. She had to make it through these three days with Jasper, just three days. They were going to be torture. Once those days were over she would be able to fall apart away from his sight and then learn how to live without him for the rest of her life.

* * *

Avoidance, that is what Jasper would associate with corn forever. Evie had managed to avoid him completely the entire day. Actually making him drive the combine, she had driven the truck but managed to just send Zoey most trips when interaction between them was necessary. During those moments, Evie had stayed in the yard far away from him.

When he had actually seen her at the beginning of the day, she hadn't even looked like their conversation the night before had affected her. Having tossed and turned all night, it pissed him off a little to see her unaffected. How many times had he almost gotten up to grab his phone to text her, but when he started he had no idea what to say.

What had happened? How had the best weekend of his life turned into a disaster so quickly? For two days, he had seen the woman he was in love with be herself and let all of her defenses down. She had been relaxed around him and was funny and animated in a way he had only seen her with others before.

For those two days, he had tried to talk about their relationship, but she always changed the subject. Maybe she wasn't ready to admit they had one, but he was. This was real, and he wanted to tell the world. She was not.

Watching the truck driving across the field, he knew it was Zoey, but within an hour she would be at her pumpkin patch. Evie would come out then, probably with Ben or Clem. Groaning as Zoey parked, he watched her climb out of the truck and climb the ladder to the combine.

After she was in the cab, she crossed her arms and said, "What the hell is going on with you two? I am sick and tired of being your go-between. Ever since you came back this tension has been there, and I am tired of it."

What to say? That they slept together, and it changed everything, but they couldn't get on the same page about their relationship. Would she understand? Probably not. She would probably just kill him.

"I don't know what you are talking about."

"That's what she said. You guys were friends, now I cannot get you within a mile of each other." Zoey gestured broadly as she spoke.

"Maybe you should talk with your sister. I have no issue with her," he said calmly.

"Don't think I haven't. If I could get her to talk I would have by now," Zoey said, then added, "I don't know what has happened between you two, it's none of my business. But you two are making my life miserable. Your constant tension is stressing me out. I don't need more stress right now. I have the pumpkin patch that I need to make a success, I am getting married in three months, and I think I am pregnant. I cannot deal with whatever you two are so mad about too. I am asking you to leave, this is her home. We can watch Clem and finish this. But I cannot keep this up."

She spun and was gone. He had no idea his and Evie's actions had affected Zoey so much. Not realizing that Zoey had so much stress in her life right now bothered him, she had never said anything about it. But he knew she was right, he didn't belong here. Evie did. Tomorrow he would leave, for Zoey. What he thought was the beginning of a great relationship was dead. There was nothing he could do to bring it back. Evie had left him no options.

Just keep working, was all he tried to think about and do, *get as much done before the end of the day*. He decided he would force Evie to talk to him when she came with the truck, if not about them, then about his leaving early. If their fighting was affecting Zoey so much, he would just leave.

Starting to plan his exit, he thought about everything that needed to be done. He would have to call his grandma and tell her he was leaving. Would she ask why? Would he actually tell her? Then he would have to see if Clem wanted to stay with Evie or Zoey. There was a lot to do before he drove away tomorrow.

The truck appeared just as he needed it—and not a minute too soon —because Evie had perfect timing for avoiding him. She was very good at it. But as he watched the truck drive across the field he thought it seemed more like Zoey than Evie's careful driving. When it stopped, Zoey jumped out of the cab. He waited for her to climb into the cab of the combine, since it was too loud to talk to her outside the machine.

When she got in she said, "I am driving this. You are on truck duty and Evie is doing the patch tonight. I can't handle you two anymore."

He could tell she was not happy about the situation, so he didn't argue, just climbed out of the cab.

When he got to the yard and had unloaded the truck, he figured he had enough time before he was needed in the field to call his grandma. Taking out his cell phone he punched in her cell number. When she answered, she sounded happy, happier than she had in months. He now hated to take that away from her and make her worry about Clem.

"Hi Grandma, it's Jasper."

"Jasper, how are you?" She sounded happy as she had every time he talked to her during her vacation.

"Okay, I guess." He tried not to let his emotions bleed into his voice.

"You sound sad, Jasper." She had always been able to read his emotions.

"It's nothing for you to worry about," he told her trying to sound more like himself.

"I worry about all my kids, Jasper."

"I am sorry, Grandma. I am leaving here tomorrow. Zoey or Evie will watch Clem until you get back. They are better at it than me, anyway," he said.

"You're good at it, you just haven't had practice. In time, you will be great with kids. Did she do something to make you leave? Is the corn done?"

"No. There is about two days left of corn and Clem has been great. She is mad at Ben for something but nothing too bad. It's me, I messed up pretty bad." Jasper leaned against the bin as he spoke.

"What did you mess up if not Clem or the harvest?"

"Just life, Grandma," he admitted.

"She's maybe to blame too, Jasper. She has a hard shell around her heart."

Caught completely off guard, Jasper pulled the phone away from his ear and looked at it. How had his grandma known what he was talking about? "What do you mean 'she?'"

"I'm not blind, Jasper. I'm talking about you and Evie. Do you think I didn't know how you feel about her? I have watched you pine after her for years. I knew you would find your Hart across the road one day." She laughed at her own joke about Evie's last name.

"What..."

"When you were young, I thought Zoey might be the one for you, but as you grew older, I knew it was Evie. I didn't push, because you needed to grow up. I knew one day it would happen," his grandma explained.

"What…" He didn't know what to say.

"She never noticed, not Evie, she doesn't look for love. I was hoping if you two could spend some time together as adults you both would notice each other." His grandmother had set him up. This whole thing was a setup.

"Well, you can stop hoping for miracles. I am not man enough to break through her shell." He wished he had been.

"Jasper, you'll never get through to her if you stop chipping now," the old lady explained.

"Cute, Grandma, but right now I have to take a break. Evie and I are not in a good place at the moment and Zoey is getting caught up in the crossfire. She has a lot of stress right now and doesn't need me adding to it."

"Zoey is not the one you should be concerned about," his grandma reminded him.

"Zoey has been great to me since Grandpa died. She's been my friend again. Now I have to be her friend and stop making her act as a buffer between Evie and me. She told me today she might be pregnant. I don't want to jeopardize that by staying."

"My Zoey? A baby!" Grandma couldn't hide the excitement in her voice.

"You cannot say I told you, it's her and Gabe's news to tell, not mine. So, act surprised when they tell you," Jasper said.

"Okay, okay, I won't tell," she promised.

"When will you be back?" he asked.

"We will head home tomorrow, so about three days."

"Good, I am leaving tomorrow morning."

"Are you ready to just let her go then? No fighting for her?"

"I think we just need a break, when I come home for the wedding maybe I can try then." He didn't even know what he would say or do then to get her back in his life.

"You do that. You deserve to be happy and so does she."

"I have to go, Grandma. I have to get back."

They said their goodbyes and Jasper hung up the phone. He just looked at it for a minute and wondered if his grandma had gone on this grand trip just to push Evie and him together. Amused, he decided if that was the plan, at least it had worked for a while.

Time to finish this day. Tomorrow he would go back to his life away from here, away from Evie. But he knew that no matter where he went, his love for her would follow.

CHAPTER 16

THE PHONE WOULD HAVE WOKEN Evie just before midnight if she had been able to sleep. Sleep was what her body craved, but more than sleep it craved Jasper. She wanted to talk to him, but she couldn't trust herself.

Grabbing the cell phone off the nightstand on the second ring, she looked at the number. Jasper. She wasn't ready to talk to him. She hadn't built up her defenses for him yet. After spending the entire day avoiding him, she still couldn't even talk to him. He would just start pulling apart her resolve and she would have to start all over again.

She watched it ring two more times in her hand. Knowing she was being childish, she just held the phone looking at his name, not daring to move for fear she would answer the call accidentally.

Zoey had told her that she had asked Jasper to leave, that Zoey was tired of being the referee between them. Her sister had told her that she was pregnant. It should have been the happiest news of Evie's year. She had hugged and danced with her sister over the new life, but the pain was still there over Jasper leaving.

Evie always knew he would leave, but now he was going even earlier for Zoey. That's the kind of man he was. He would probably be going tomorrow. How many years would it be before she saw him again?

The name appeared again. He was calling again. Again, she watched it for the length of four rings, then it disappeared. No voicemail. It was after the second call that a message came pinged.

JASPER: It's Clem, I need help.

EVIE WAS out of bed and out of the house in an instant. What was wrong with Clem? Did she have an accident? It took less than five minutes and she was at his front door. Jasper was standing waiting for her.

"What's wrong with Clem?" she asked breathless from her run.

"I don't know. She won't leave the bathroom. She's been in there for hours."

He was in jeans and a T-shirt. He looked so good, too good. Evie felt frumpy as she climbed the stairs to the second floor, maybe she should have changed out of her pajama pants and top before coming over. But no, she was here for Clem, not Jasper.

As Jasper followed she said, "I will figure it out. You stay downstairs."

She saw the hurt in his eyes and wished she hadn't been so sharp with him. He was worried about his cousin.

Knocking on the door she said, "Clem? It's me, Evie. Can I come in?"

"No," said the girl behind the door.

"What's wrong?" Evie sat down against the closed door. She was going to be here a while. Teenage girls could stay in rooms for hours, at least Zoey could.

"Nothing," came from behind the door.

"Is it something Jasper did?" Evie started there.

"No," the girl said behind the door. "But he is leaving tomorrow. He is leaving me too."

"We always knew he would leave, but he will come back. Because he loves you," Evie said to herself as much as to the girl, though she knew he didn't love her, it had just been a favor to a friend for him.

"I know, but everyone leaves me. Not just him," Clem said.

"He is not leaving you, he works in Minneapolis, he'll come home again all the time. Maybe you can talk to him about coming back more often?"

How was she going to convince this girl something she couldn't convince herself of? Why was she convinced that when he left, she would never see him again? Because he was leaving her.

"It's not just Jasper, Grandma left," Clem's voice was quiet as it come through the door.

"She is coming back in a week, then she won't leave again for a long time. And if she does, you know she'll come back, every time," Evie stated.

"Grandpa left," the girl mumbled.

"He didn't want to. He wanted to be here with you." Evie hurt for the girl who lost her grandpa to young.

"My dad left. He never came back." She sniffled as she spoke of the man who she hadn't seen in over eleven years.

"Eddie was a bastard, you know that. He didn't deserve to be in your life. The only good thing he ever did was leaving you here," Evie said.

It was the truth. Clem was much better off without his presence in her life.

"Ben says he doesn't want to marry me anymore," Clem admitted.

Evie chuckled at that, young love was fickle. "Forget about Ben, there are a ton of guys out there to saddle yourself with him so early."

"How can you say that? He's your son." Clem's voice held a note of shock.

"I can say that because I can see you two as friends, nothing more. You two have a lot of growing up to do before you decide you want more. And while you are growing up, there are other boys out there that might be better than Ben for you. And if not, then you can see what more there is. Just give it time."

Evie hoped that the young girl was understanding, because the more she talked, the more things were becoming clear about her and

Jasper. For weeks, she had wondered why she had never seen him as anything but a kid until one day he was a man. Now she saw that they both had to grow up before they would even see each other in that light. But she also knew that there was no going back to how it was before.

"I guess."

"Are you ready to come out then?" Evie asked, noticing that Jasper had creeped up the stairs and was watching her. She wondered how long he had been listening, probably too long.

"No," said the girl.

"You do know that no matter who leaves you and stays gone or comes back, there will always be someone here for you. You have me, Zoey, Gabe, and now Della's moving back. There are so many people here for you that love you that you're going to be begging to get away from us to go to college one day."

She closed her eyes so she didn't have to see Jasper as she leaned back against the door.

"Ever since you were a baby I have thought of you as my baby too. You know that, right? You are very important to me. I love you very much, Clementine."

Evie wasn't ready when the door flew open behind her. That's how she found herself lying flat on her back on the bathroom floor staring up at the twelve-year-old standing over her.

"Get in here," the girl whispered.

Evie pulled her legs in the room and Clem slammed the door shut behind her.

"You could have warned me about the door." Evie laughed.

Evie sat on the floor and leaned against the vanity. Evie's heart ached as the teen slid down the door to a sitting position. It had been hard for Evie as a teenager and it looked like Clem's years weren't going any easier.

"I got my period today," Clem admitted.

Evie reached out and pulled her into a tight hug. "Welcome."

No wonder Clem had been an emotional wreck this week. It was a lot to go through for a girl, and worse when the only adult in the house was a guy. Squeezing her one more time she let the girl go.

Clem leaned back against the door and looked around the room. "To what?"

Evie laughed. "To womanhood. That sounded cheesy even as I said it, sorry."

"Is it always this way? Like your emotions are out of whack?" Clem asked.

"Yes, but you get used to it. You learn the signs and figure out how to deal with it," Evie said.

"What about the other stuff?" She pointed at her crotch.

"You get used to that too. You never get it under control one hundred percent, but you figure it out. Don't let it all scare you. It's all natural and your body was made for it."

Evie didn't think she was doing a good job of explaining everything to Clem. The last time she had had this conversation was with Zoey, so many years ago.

"Why does it even have to happen?" Clem asked the age-old question.

"So that one day, you can have a baby. And on that day, you will look at that little baby and say to it that it was all worth it for you." Evie admitted with a grin, remembering Ben as a tiny baby. He was worth everything she had been through.

"All this for a baby?" Clem asked incredulously.

"There are other great things about being a woman, but that is the big one." Evie wasn't going to go into that with the girl, some things she didn't need to know yet.

"Not really a superpower," Clem stated.

"It can be. Tomorrow you should ask Zoey how she used to get out of class by just saying she had lady problems. I didn't realize the potential benefits until after I was out of school, but Zoey got out of a semester of gym class. I'm sure she'd be happy to tell you all about it and maybe has more secrets that I don't know about." Evie laughed at her sister's antics, knowing she would love to share her knowledge with the younger girl.

"I will," she said with a smile.

"Do you have what you need?" Evie asked.

"Yeah, Grandma bought some stuff last summer. So, I am okay."

"Okay, if you need more, just call and I will get you more," Evie said. "Are you ready to leave this room?"

"Yes." They both got to their feet. Clem hugged her, and she hugged the girl back. "Thanks for coming. I couldn't talk to Jasper about it."

Opening the door Evie said, "I understand. You need to go to bed though, it's way past midnight."

"Can you not tell Jasper? He is leaving tomorrow anyway. He doesn't need to know," Clem asked.

"I will not tell," she lied. Jasper needed to know that there was nothing seriously wrong with his cousin. Not that she would disclose the rest of their conversation, because he didn't need know about that.

"Okay, goodnight, Evie."

"Goodnight, Clem."

Watching as Clem went into her bedroom, Evie turned and saw Jasper at the top of the stairway.

He mouthed, "What?"

Indicating for him to go downstairs, she followed behind admiring his backside as she went and remembered what it looked like without the T-shirt on. When she got the bottom of the stairs, she pulled on her shoes and was grabbing her coat when he huffed in disbelief, "Where are you going?"

Quickly she looked up the stairs and was relieved not to see Clem.

"Outside. She can still hear us down here."

It was almost true. Maybe if Clem's bedroom door was open and she was listening for them. But with her door shut she shouldn't. But Evie couldn't be inside alone with Jasper. She needed more space between them than that the small living room provided.

Putting on her coat, she watched him grab his and pull on his boots. She felt him behind her as she walked out of the house and onto the lawn.

"What is going on with Clem?" he demanded in confusion.

"She got her period today," she said, and as with most men, that shut him up. "She needed to talk to someone who had been through it. Not you."

"Isn't she a little young for all that?" he asked.

"I was younger than her when I got mine. So no, she is not too young," Evie explained.

"She thought everyone was leaving her?" The sadness in his voice made her long to hug him, comfort him.

"Yes, and no. She is missing Grandma Betty and Grandpa Bill, but she knows why they are gone and that they didn't leave her behind on purpose," Evie said.

"And now me."

"She always knew you were going back to your life," Evie said.

Just like Evie had known. It didn't make it any easier when it actually happened. Didn't make her sad that it was happening.

With obvious surprise, he asked, "Is that what you think? That I am just going back to my life like nothing's changed?"

"Jasper, this is not about us. It's about Clem."

"You could come back with me," he said, taking a step closer to her.

"I have no place in the city, Jasper, that is not my life," she said taking a step back from him to keep her distance. If he got too close, her resolve would melt.

"Could we just try?" His voice made her want things that she couldn't have.

"It's never going to work, Jasper." She backed up another step. "Go back to your life, Jasper, forget about me." She turned and walked away.

She heard him yell from behind her. "I have been trying to forget about you since I was fifteen. You are all I have ever wanted. I want you to know that. I want you to think about that when I am gone."

Just keep walking, she demanded of herself, *don't turn around*. He needed to go back to his life and forget about her. He would never be happy here with her, and she could never be happy in his life. No matter how much she loved him.

By the time she had crossed the road separating the properties, she knew he wasn't following. She was alone in the dark. Had she wanted him to follow? Yes, she longed for him to follow and demand they find a way to make it work. Another part of her was glad she didn't have to face him again today. Tomorrow he would be gone.

CHAPTER 17

THE CAR WAS ALREADY PACKED before Clem came down for breakfast. Jasper had been up most of the night, unable to sleep after his talk with Evie, so he had packed and loaded the car. Now he was just waiting for the teen to eat and get on the bus.

Watching Evie last night sitting against the bathroom door, talking to Clem about leaving and staying, it hit him then that she didn't want him to leave. But she also couldn't make him stay and his suggestion that she move to the city with him wasn't going to work. He had to decide if he wanted to stay at a job he loved or move back here and be with the woman he loved.

"How are you this morning?" Jasper asked his cousin as he started the ancient coffee pot brewing.

"Fine." Clem grabbed a box of cereal from the cupboard.

"Is there anything you need from me?" He sat down across from her.

"Like what?" She looked at him in confusion, stopping mid cereal pour.

"You know…" he began, stumbling over any of the products that she might need, that he had no idea about. "Lady stuff." Yup, he was an adult.

"I don't." Her cereal bowl was only half full but she didn't seem to notice as she added milk.

"I'm leaving today and you will be staying with Zoey until Grandma comes back."

This morning he had talked to Zoey and she had seemed happy to take the teen for a few days. There had been no way he would ask Evie to take her, because that would involve speaking to her.

"You're running away?" Clem asked between bites of cereal.

"What?" He looked up the preteen on the other side of the table.

"You're running away," she repeated.

"What am I running away from?" he asked.

"Evie. I have eyes," she said she pointed to her brown ones.

"What have your eyes seen?"

He wanted to know. They had barely been together and mostly only when the kids were fighting and preoccupied with their own drama.

"How you look at her when she is not looking. She looks at you too." Clem had seen way too much.

"I am not running away. I am leaving because we are not getting along right now. It's best for all of us for me to leave right now," he explained. It was true, he had to decide if his job was worth the loss of his heart, or his Hart to be exact.

"Are you coming back?" Clem asked.

"I don't know if Evie wants me to."

He knew he was coming back for Zoey's wedding. By then he hoped he would have everything figured out and know what he had to offer her.

"Evie doesn't always know what's good for her. Grandpa used to say that and it's true," Clem said.

When the bus horn blasted, Clem grabbed her backpack, saying a quick goodbye and ran out of the house. Leaving it silent in her wake.

Jasper's mind drifted back to Evie sitting against the door, talking and fiddling with her hands. Jasper had often watched her slide her wedding ring off only to try it on her other fingers as she talked. It would fit on her pinky, then only halfway down the middle and pointer fingers and then she would try the thumb. It would only go down a small bit and she would stare it at for a little. Then take it off and slide it back on her ring finger. He had watched her do it many times over the years. She always did it when she had nothing to do with her hands during conversations.

Sometimes she would just spin it with her thumb, or with her other hand. But last night she had just looked at her hands and touched the spot where her ring had sat, then back to looking at her hands. The ring had been gone. At the time he thought it was because of him, but after their conversation he didn't know.

Well, he was going to give her until the wedding, then he would be relentless until he broke down every wall she had. Even if it took a lifetime. She would be his one day and be his forever.

CHAPTER 18

THE CORN HAD BEEN HARVESTED and was in bins, pumpkin season was over, and the fields had been cultivated for the next year. Even all the vegetable gardens had been prepped for winter. November was here and most days were spent at the mansion cleaning, painting, and repairing for the wedding and for Della to move in. Evie was exhausted, but every day she went back to do more for her sisters and their dreams.

Della had moved in with Evie within days of Jasper's leaving. But with the help of carpenter Chad, they had made huge progress on the house and Della hoped to move in by Thanksgiving.

Zoey had a way of convincing everybody else do her bidding. Once she set her mind to something, she moved heaven and earth to get it done. The house would be in shape by the wedding. Not all of it, but enough to hold the wedding of her dreams.

It had been fun for Evie, having her sisters around all the time, but she got tired of them also. Zoey was so happy and Della had the world by the tail. Though she had been fired a month ago, Della was well on her way to opening her own law office in Birch Cove. She worked at the mansion during the day and read law books by night, learning more about family law.

As happy as she was for her sisters, Evie's own life was falling apart. Jasper was gone, he hadn't texted, called, or even written a letter to her. He was completely out of her life. She would hear this and that from Clem about him, but since Betty returned, Clem had stayed at her own house more than usual.

It had been four days since Evie had given her ring to Gabe and Zoey. She had gone over there on Gabe's day off. She had texted them she wanted to see them, gone were the days of just showing up.

Zoey had let her in and she had sat them down at the table. Pulling the ring out of her pocket and unsure of how to broach the subject she started with, "I don't know if you guys have picked out a ring for Zoey yet ..."

"Yes, when I got the engagement ring," Gabe informed her with suspicion.

Zoey couldn't stop staring at the ring and immediately understood what Evie was trying to offer. "I don't want your ring, Evie. It's yours."

Evie looked at it too. "You mean it represents my bad marriage?"

Zoey looked up at Evie's eyes. "Maybe."

Evie laid the ring on the table between them. "That's not what I see when I see it. Yes, I used it for my disaster of a marriage, but that is not the ring's fault. Greg never bought me a ring, so I used this one. I already had it from when Grandma Connor died as the oldest granddaughter."

She continued, "When I see it, I remember Grandma Connor. She died before you were born, Zoey, but she was a great woman. To be honest, she hated this ring. She wanted a flashier ring when her and Grandpa got married, but Grandpa had already gotten this one without asking. She told me that right before she died. I asked her why she never got a different ring when they had the money." She looked at the plain gold band.

Swallowing back her tears, she continued, "She told me this was the ring that the man who loved her bought for her, and she would wear it because she loved him. This ring represents real love, and that no matter what life brings you, that love remains. I had the honor of wearing this ring even though my marriage did not have that love. I want you to wear it because yours does. It's not about how much you love the ring. It's about how much you love the man who gave it to you."

Hoping that her sister saw the beauty in the ring, that Evie always had. Not just the symbol it was to a disaster of a marriage. Evie couldn't bear to look at it alone and cold on the table, missing it from her hand.

Zoey picked up the plain band and read 'Connor' that was engraved on the inside. Zoey had never known her grandparents on their mom's side as they were gone before she had been born. It felt good for her to have a little piece of it.

She wiped her tears and got up. "It's yours if you want it. If you don't want to use it has a wedding ring, just keep it. You keep it and hand it down to your kids one day."

She left before they even said anything. There was nothing they could say to make her take the ring back with her, because she had to let it go.

With it out of her possession there was a small relief, a lightness that she no longer had to carry on a legacy that she couldn't anymore. In fact, maybe she'd never had been able to. But her sister had the love the ring represented.

In the days that followed, Zoey hadn't returned the ring, nor said if she would wear it. But it didn't matter to Evie, because she needed to be rid of it. Needed to be free of the reminder of her past even if she loved that ring.

Since Evie had taken the ring off the day Jasper had accused her of hiding behind it, she hadn't missed it too much. That had been weeks ago. Or was it years? She couldn't tell anymore. Time had no meaning these days even if she still sometimes felt the ache of his absence.

The master bedroom in the mansion had been cleaned, swept, the edges taped, and Della had even started painting before Evie made it to the bedroom. She had known they were tackling this room today— the room Jasper had kissed her in. Was that all it took to make her not want to step in the door? Pushing through the heartache, she walked into the room. Della had chosen off-white paint for the walls since the wainscoting and molding were already stained dark and the house just needed something light.

"You started without me," Evie accused.

"I couldn't wait forever for you," Della said, Evie could tell her mood wasn't great today.

"Sorry," Evie said. "How is it going?"

"You can see how it is going," Della spat out.

"What is wrong with you today, Della?" Evie asked.

Her sister had been excited about her move back and about opening the law firm. This was the first time she had seen her older sister anything but happy about her future.

"Evie." She turned around with her brush in hand. "I don't want to go to your pity party today. I have spent too long there."

"What does that mean?" Evie was taken aback. She had worked so hard to keep her emotions under control around her sisters.

"What does that mean? It means all you do is mope and sulk and do the poor me dance. It is getting on everybody's nerves." She put the brush down and stood with her hands on her hips. Only Della would wear designer jeans and a blouse to paint, and of course, high-heeled sandals.

"Everybody?" Evie demanded. Nobody had said a thing to her.

"Everybody, Evie. Zoey won't say anything because you were so good to her when she broke up with Gabe. You were a rock." Della ran her fingers through her now red hair, that had been her first change when she moved back to town.

"I was a rock, you weren't around. She had it bad," Evie threw back at her.

"Well, the rock isn't very sturdy now, Evie. Why don't you just go to him? There is nothing keeping you here that can't be found there."

"Who?" Evie questioned.

"Jasper Reed! You have been pining for him since he left. And from what Zoey said, before he left," Della stated.

"You have no idea what you are talking about." Evie didn't even what to talk about it with her sister.

"You think that we are all blind? That we didn't see how he chased you? And that you just sent him packing for no reason," Della said as she started to pace the room.

"No reason? He lives in the middle of the city. I live on a farm," Evie explained.

"Why?" Della demanded.

"Why what?"

"Why is that farm out there so important?" Della was still pacing the bedroom.

"It's where I live. I work that land," Evie said as if it were obvious. Her life was this land. It always had been.

"Can you work other land? Does it have to be *that* land? Can Evie only farm the land her daddy gave her?" Della challenged.

"I could farm anywhere." Evie shook her head. That was not how it happened and Della knew it. Evie worked hard for everything she got.

"Then, why don't you? Get a farm closer to Minneapolis, be with Jasper, he can drive into town for work. You don't need Birch Cove. Zoey can take care of the farms. You can come help out on the weekends, it's only a two-hour drive," Della said.

"It's not that easy, Della, Ben is here and his school and his life," Evie argued.

"It is if you try, but you won't try. You say he lives too far away, that it can't be changed. But it can be changed, you just won't try. There are even schools there, Evie, nice ones. Ben will make friends and be happy any place you take him," Della said.

"There is more to it than that," Evie said.

"Oh, you mean your shitty marriage. I assume he knows about that, he lived across the road the whole time," Della reminded her.

"You don't know what you are talking about." Evie had never talked to Della about her marriage, ever.

"I don't know what? That he used to beat you? That he talked down to you every chance he got? That he hated Ben, who was only a baby. Or that Ben wasn't even his." Della's voice had dropped, her face creasing in pain as she revealed the truths Evie had always thought she had hidden from others. She had tried at least.

"How..." Evie stammered.

"You were arm candy to him. He enjoyed having a date to all the dances so all the other girls wouldn't hang on him. You were his cover, but he never touched you," Della said.

"You don't know what you are talking about," Evie tried to deflect Della's assumptions. Della could not have any idea.

"I saw him, Evie." Della stopped pacing. "I was at the university that year also. Maybe I was there doing postgraduate work, but the parties were the same. I saw him with guys. It made a lot of pieces fit about your relationship. Then you were pregnant, and he married you. You gave him the excuse to come back here and be the football hero again. But that didn't happen did it? He was already a has-been by that time."

"You knew all along?" Evie whispered in disbelief.

"Yes, so don't act all 'poor me' to me, Evie, you chose that one. Dad would never have made you marry him. Dad hated Greg," Della said. Her pacing had started again.

"You're right. I made a mistake," Evie admitted.

"Yes, and you've regretted it for eleven years. Poor Evie had a bad marriage. Poor Evie had to quit college and have a baby. Poor Evie got to farm with her dad for years. Poor Evie has a man who's had a crush on her for years actually fall in love with her. Poor Evie, my heart bleeds for your pain," Della shouted at her.

"It isn't that easy. I didn't know what Dad would do when I came home pregnant," Evie admitted. It had been such a confusing time, but she knew now she had messed up.

"He would have done the exact same thing he actually did: fixed up a house and moved you close to home. Close to him. You could never do anything wrong, Evie," Della hadn't ceased her pacing back and forth in the small room.

"I didn't know he would be so understanding about it. I thought he would blow his top and send me away. I got lucky," Evie said watching her movements.

"Sure it was luck! Once again you got lucky, and I got shit," Della said, stopping to look out the window.

"What are you talking about?" Evie demanded.

"Did he ever ask if you wanted to put the baby up for adoption?" Della questioned still looking out the window.

"No, he said he wanted me to keep him. Right away, from the first time I told him," Evie said, remembering how supportive her dad was about the entire thing. How he knew all the right things to say and when to say them.

"You're lucky, Evie. You never even knew how lucky you were. You just took it for granted that you got to take your son home." Evie started to shake her head, but Della barreled on. "Evie, you did! And I know it was hard being a single mom, but then to hear you complain about having to raise your son? That you were lucky enough?" Della was still looking out the window. But Evie could tell she was holding back tears.

"Yes, I was lucky. But it has been hard to raise him on my own, Della," Evie said, wanting to pull her sister into her arms.

Della turned from the window and shouted, "Do you know what is hard, Evie? Hard is not taking your son home. Hard is letting someone else raise him. Hard is never getting to see him again."

"What are you talking about?" Evie questioned her older sister.

"I am talking about how you got it all, Evie. You got a house, a job, a son. And all you do is constantly complain about it," she continued to yell.

"I do not constantly complain about it! And why would you care? You have a career and a great life in the city," Evie retorted feeling her own anger rise.

"And I would give it all up for one minute with my baby, to take her home like you got to take yours home," Della said shaking her head, not yelling anymore.

Della pushed past her and out the bedroom door. Evie tried to grab her arm but missed. Turning, she followed her and called out, "What? I've always been with you, when did you have a baby?"

Della stopped but didn't say anything. Then said, "You weren't the only one who got knocked up freshman year. Maybe that's why Dad was in such a hurry to get Zoey in the Army. I had her the summer I turned sixteen. And I am considered the smart one."

"What happened?" Evie's heart broke for her sister.

"A boy noticed me, I said yes, and then he walked away. Same old story. But Dad made me put her up for adoption, he never made you do that," Della said.

"Where was I?" Evie thought back to those years, sure she was self-absorbed like all kids, but she would have noticed that!

"I stayed at school. Took summer school, didn't come home again for years. Not until you brought home Ben," Della explained quietly, looking at the wall and not at Evie.

"I didn't notice." Evie looked back on those years and all she could remember was Della was in college. Not one memory of her being home. Maybe Evie's own graduation, but no other moments did she remember seeing her sister. Why hadn't she realized that before?

"We were never a close family, Evie," Della said.

Evie want to argue with her, yes they were. But it was true, their dad hadn't made time with his children a priority in his life. As a result the sisters had spent years letting the distance stay between them.

"How old is she? Have you ever met her?" Evie asked about the niece she never knew she had.

"Seventeen, she was born on my birthday, my sweet sixteen. I have never seen her since I gave her up. She has a family that isn't me." Della's voice was empty as she stated the heartbreaking facts.

"Why didn't you ever tell me?" Evie asked.

"You were fourteen, Evie, a kid. Once you had grown up, time had passed, and it just never came up." Della started down the stairs again. "I am going for a ride, don't tell Zoey about this, she doesn't need to know."

"I won't," Evie agreed, hoping that Della would tell their little sister herself one day. One day soon.

When Della got to the front door she turned around and said, "Don't 'poor me' about how bad your life is anymore, Evie. You got more than some of us ever got."

They stared into each other's eyes for a minute and then the door burst open and Zoey breezed in. "Is everybody ready to work?"

Della turned to her and said, "No, I'm leaving." Then she was out the door.

Zoey turned to Evie and asked, "What was that about? Should we just let her go?"

Evie wiped her eyes with her sleeve and sat down on the top step. "Just let her go. She needs space."

Evie stared at the door her sister had slammed shut, her sister who had just shattered everything Evie had even known. Sitting on the top step of the grand staircase, she looked back on her career-orientated sister. Were there signs Evie had missed? Did their father really make her put her baby up for adoption but not Evie's? Did he do it because Della was sixteen compared to Evie's eighteen? Did Della actually just let her baby be adopted out? Without a fight? Is that why Della had never shown any interest in having kids of her own? So many questions and no answers.

Zoey walked slowly up the stairs and then sat next to her sister, putting her arm around her. "What happened?"

Evie just let the tears fall as she said, "Della made me see that I didn't fuck up my life when I got pregnant. That having that baby was a gift. Not everyone gets to keep that gift."

Zoey just sat beside Evie as she got her emotions under control. It was all too much. She had let another sister down so badly. First Zoey by never being there for her when she was in the Army, and now Della because she had been too young to understand what was happening. Was she letting herself down by letting Jasper go?

"Are you tired of my pity party too?" Evie asked Zoey.

"It has been no fun, but my pity party was worse, so I put up with it," Zoey said with a laugh.

"I'm sorry," Evie whispered, wishing she could say more.

"I blame Jasper," Zoey assured her.

"It wasn't him, it was me. I messed it all up. He asked me to move to Minneapolis with him," Evie said.

Zoey pushed her sister away and looked at her. "What? Are you going to?"

"I can't, you know that, the farm is here. I can't work from an apartment," Evie explained, Zoey would at least understand, more than Della would.

"Of course you can. Well, not exactly. But you can farm here and live there. There would be times you will have to stay here, but there are times you could just be there. Rain days, all of winter, and slow times when I can handle the work myself. Jasper can drive out during the busy times for planting and harvest. We can make it work. Next year, Clem and Ben will be an even bigger help than this year. We can hire a high school or college kid for the summer. This is not that big of a hurdle." Zoey was getting excited about the thought, then added, "And you can do all the Minneapolis farmer's markets, you'll live there."

"You sound like Della, though she said to get a farm closer to Minneapolis," Evie said.

"That could work also, we could expand. Maybe rent out the farmland and just concentrate on the veggies," Zoey said pulling her into a hug again.

"You guys make it sound easy," Evie admitted as Zoey's grip loosened.

"You make it sound impossible. It's not. We can make it work, we always do." Zoey hugged her again.

"What about his age? He's so young." Evie hated talking about Jasper's age, because it made her feel old when she did.

"Age, Evie? Is that all you have? That's all you cared about with Gabe and me too, and we are making it work."

Zoey was thirteen years younger than Gabe and Evie had been worried about the difference when they first started dating. It had been one of her major reasons for not liking Gabe when he first came around.

"It's different," Evie argued.

"He is the same age I was when I met Gabe, and you are years younger than Gabe is. Age is in your head, Evie. Nobody is going to look at you to and say, she is a lot older than him," Zoey said.

"They might."

Zoey laughed at her. "My fiancé once got a lecture that age didn't matter in a relationship as long as both people were happy. I think that advice also works for the person who gave it."

Evie remembered giving that speech to a stubborn Gabe after he had broken up with Zoey due to his being too old for her, or so he thought. Evie had thought it also, until she realized that her sister loved the guy no matter what his age was. They had worked their way through it and they were very happy together now.

"What else do you have? What other arguments do you got in there?" Zoey tapped on Evie's head.

Evie leaned her head on her sister's shoulder and whispered, "I think I am pregnant."

"What?" Zoey shouted. "When? How? You weren't going to tell me? Does Jasper know?"

"I just realized it recently, but I didn't want it to be real. That sounded bad. I am excited to have Jasper's baby, but I don't want him to be with me only because I am having his baby," Evie admitted.

She had suspected it since the night she went over and talked to Clem about getting her period. As they had talked, she had realized she had missed more than one of her periods since August. The more she looked back at that time she realized they had not used protection that first time in the combine. Every other time they had, but the damage was already done.

"We are going to have babies together," Zoey said in awe of the possibility. "Have you been sick?"

"No, just tired. Maybe if I had been sick, I would have realized it sooner."

"Did it happen during your trip to Minneapolis? I was pretty sneaky about that one. When neither of you said no to staying at Jasper's house, I knew something was up. So, that means you're about four weeks along. I am seven weeks this week. So, a month behind me?" Zoey did the math in her head.

"Yes, but we'll be more than a month and a half apart. You're actually behind me." Evie hated to admit the truth, but it was going to be known soon enough.

"What? When? Really?" Zoey asked all excited again. Pulling out her phone and looking at the calendar, Zoey said, "Right around the time of Grandpa Bills funeral? That's when it had to be. And I thought that you were just taking his passing hard."

Evie nodded in agreement. "It just happened, we didn't plan it." She felt her cheeks getting red and covered them with her hands.

Zoey laughed at her and jumped up. "Too late for blushing, Evie."

Then Zoey headed down the stairs and Evie asked, "Don't we have to paint?"

Zoey laughed again and said, "Us pregnant people don't have to paint. Gabe and Chad can do it. We have to go get you ready to see Jasper."

"Is he coming up?" Evie hadn't heard anything about him coming back.

"Nope, Evie, you are going to him. But we have to clean you up a little first."

Evie got up from her spot on the top step, taking one step at a time. That was how she was going to do this. One step at a time closer to Jasper.

CHAPTER 19

THE DAY HAD BEEN STRESSFUL. It had taken Jasper almost three weeks to get caught up on the work he had missed while he was harvesting corn for his grandfather. Work had kept his mind off Evie to a degree, but she still was there. Now his workload had slowed and he could go home at a decent hour, but now he hated it there.

Everything reminded him of Evie. The bed that they had slept in during the farmer's market weekend. The one night he had been able to hold her in his arms the entire night. The couch that they had snuggled on and eaten delivered Chinese food. She was everywhere, and he sometimes thought he could even smell her.

He had been reduced to watching the home improvement shows she loved and now knew all the shows and the hosts' names. He had found a hair elastic on the floor last week and had had it in his pocket every day as he worked, touching it when he needed to feel close to her.

At this point he didn't know how he would make it to Christmas. It was just over a week until Thanksgiving, he would be able to see her then. But what if it was too soon, and he just spooked her again? Then what?

Leaning forward, he picked up the contract he had received today from the coffee table, only to put it down again to witness the great reveal at the end of the show he was watching. He knew he had watched too many of these, because he was thinking about putting in hardwood floors at Evie's house. And maybe new paint. And of course, they would need new furniture now that Della would be taking most of hers. He sighed and leaned back on the couch, now he was remodeling her house in his mind. This was getting bad.

His phone buzzed from the coffee table with a text. He leaned forward and grabbed the phone to read it. His heart flipped in his chest, it was Evie.

Evie: Are you home?

Jasper: Yes.

Was she going to call, talk to him for the first time in weeks? What did she want to talk about? Was she calling about them or something about the farm or his grandma? He sat holding his phone, waiting. There was a knock on his door and he thought about ignoring it, he had an important phone call coming in and he knew nobody that was coming over. He needed to concentrate on the phone.

Since the phone still hadn't rung, he decided he could move the knocker along quickly, so he jumped up, and without looking through the peephole, flung the door open.

Over the years, many people had gotten lost in the building looking for certain apartments and had knocked on his door. So, this wasn't necessarily a new thing, just something that happened from time to time.

When the door opened, he realized it wasn't a lost visitor. It was Evie, standing there in his hallway.

She was wearing the blue dress from the funeral under a long jacket. It was still just as short, but maybe a bit tighter? He now knew it was Della's, that Evie had not had a dress to wear to the funeral and had borrowed this one. She still looked amazing in it. Her hair was loose, longer, and less curly than the last time he had seen it down.

"Can I come in?" she asked. He could tell she was nervous.

He was just staring at her, he hadn't even invited her in. Standing back, he let her in. All he wanted to do was touch her and take her into his arms. But he forced himself to keep his distance since he didn't want to scare her away.

"Are you waiting for a call?" she asked.

He was still clinching his phone in his hand. Waiting for her call.

"No," he admitted now that she was here.

Placing the phone on the coffee table, he offered her a seat. She left the jacket on but unbuttoned it as she perched on the edge of the couch.

"How are you Evie?"

"I am fine, just… Jasper, I have been selfish and mean to you, you didn't deserve that. I wish that I had noticed you years ago. I don't know how that would have turned out. Probably badly. I never noticed you as more than the kid next door, Zoey's friend, Betty and Bill's grandson," she said.

As she spoke, she fiddled with her ring finger. The ring may have been gone, but she still fidgeted with her fingers when she was nervous. He wondered if she had stopped wearing it the night she had talked to Clem. If she never put it back on what did that mean?

"Evie, my grandma said I needed to grow up. Now I have," Jasper said just looking at her, taking her in.

"You talked to your grandma about us?" Evie asked, a blush in her cheeks. Jasper realized she was probably embarrassed by the possibility since Betty was like a grandma to Evie too.

"No, not really. I only her that I was leaving early. She guessed it was about you." He sat down near her on the couch.

"She knows?" Evie's green eyes went wide.

"Yes, she's known all along. She said I found my Hart across the road years ago. I just had to grow up before I could go get it. She went on her vacation so we would have to spend time together. She's pretty cunning." He chuckled.

"She's not the only one. Zoey planned the Minneapolis trip so we could be alone," Evie said.

"I guess both their plans worked." He smiled at her.

She shook her head. "Jasper, I am here to apologize, so don't stop me. I am sorry for letting my head interfere with my heart. I spent too much time when we were together trying to convince myself why we shouldn't be together. I should have spent the time we had being happy and with you."

"What were your reasons?" he asked, taking her nervous hands into his so she would stop fidgeting.

"One is you are too young, but Zoey said age doesn't matter when it comes to love."

"She's right. I don't care how old you are, Evie. I never have." He lifted her hands and kissed the backs of them.

"Two is that you live and work here, in the city. And Ben and I are out at the farm. It seemed impossible to get over that one. But both my sisters pointed out that with their help we can make it work. I can live here and drive out to the farm when needed, and you can come on the weekends. Or we can find land closer to Minneapolis and Zoey can work in Birch Cove and I can farm the new place. Ben seems willing to move anyplace as long as we go back to the farm often. So many options. All of which I was unable to see until they pointed them out. Sometimes I am bad at planning." She was talking fast, nervously.

"You would move for me?" he asked in surprise. His Evie had changed over the last month.

"Yes, we can live here with you in the city, but I would rather have a farm somewhere. I don't want to give up the farmer's markets, but I can give up the grain farming," she said.

"You would give it all up for me?" He knew how much the farming meant to her. "Why?"

"Because I love you. I love you too much to lose you. I have been without you for three weeks and I don't want to live without you anymore."

He pulled her onto his lap and hungrily kissed her. She answered the kiss with a matching hunger. He slid the jacket off her body and it landed half on the coffee table and half on the floor. Running his hands up her back, he laughed and said, "Your dress is not zipped."

"It doesn't fit anymore. But I knew you liked it. I needed everything I had to get you back." She continued kissing his face.

Stopping her kissing, he held her face in his hands, kissed her lightly on the lips and said, "You never needed to get me back, you had me the whole time. I just needed you to realize it."

"You didn't come back," she whispered.

"I was coming back for you at Thanksgiving. I thought that was enough time for you to figure things out. If it wasn't, I was going to chip at that wall until I finally broke through it. I was just waiting." He kissed her again, biting her lip gently, making her moan in his arms.

He pulled away a moment and said, "I have something to show you before I make love to you."

He reached into the paperwork on the coffee table, lifting a sheet of paper and handing it to her. He loved the creases of confusion on her forehead. She read it again, her lips moving as she read it to herself the second time.

"What is this?" she finally asked.

"This is a lease for a building on Main Street, in Birch Cove. I am going to open my own accounting office in town. I can drive there from your farm. For months my job hasn't been as fulfilling as it used to be, before I realized how much I was missing by being away from home. Because that's what Birch Cove is, home. I just hope that you want me there."

He took the paper from her hand and threw it on the coffee table again.

Evie's eyes widened at his declaration. "More than anything I want you there. I want you everywhere and anywhere."

He easily lifted her into his arms and carried her to his bedroom. Putting her on her feet he peeled off the beautiful dress and watched it drop to the floor at her feet, like he had dreams of so many times. He laid her on the bed and just looked at her. He was never going to get tired of her body, and planned to spend a lot of time touching it, remembering the feel of it.

He felt her unbuttoning his shirt as he touched her body for the first time in weeks. He loved the feel of her hands, almost as much as he loved his hands on her. She peeled his pants and underwear off in one motion and he couldn't wait a moment longer. He leaned over to his nightstand and grabbed a condom. She grabbed it out of his hand and threw it across the room.

"We don't need that," she whispered. "Just you and me."

He was too far gone to argue as she took him in her hand and guided him into her wet folds. She was soft and wet and she shifted until he was fully inside her and there was no stopping either of them until they peaked together.

When he was able to move again, he gathered her into his arms and nuzzled her neck. "God, I love you, Evie Hart. When will you marry me?"

She stiffened and said, "Marry you?"

"You need to make an honest man out of me. And you have a kid in the house that will notice his mom sleeping with a man every night. You have an example to set. You have to marry me, for Ben," he said and shifted her so he was looking into her green eyes.

"Marry you?" she said again.

He shifted out of the bed pulled her until she too was standing. Then he got down on one knee and still holding her hand, said, "I do not have a ring but, Evangelina Connor Hart, will you marry me?"

He watched her sink to her knees as she chanted, "Yes, yes, yes."

"I love you, Evie. I knew I loved you when I saw you standing in a wheat field at sunset. I knew you were the one—everyone else is a pale comparison. I could barely keep my hands off you after that day." He pulled her into his arms.

"I didn't notice anything. But I had been trying not to notice you since the funeral. After that day, I wanted you to touch me again and to stay away from me at the same time," she said.

"Why did you ask me to have sex with you?" he asked.

She blushed and ducked her head. "For all the reasons I told you, I wanted to learn about sex and I wanted to start dating."

"Why me?" He needed to know.

"You were the first man who had ever made me feel wanted and desired. I wanted you to touch me. I had never met anyone I wanted to have touch me."

Almost unconsciously, her own fingers had embarked on an exploration of his body at her admission, because he was the first man she had wanted to touch.

"I loved teaching you about sex, but I didn't have to," Jasper said, touching her wheat colored hair.

"I know, you're a nice guy," Evie whispered.

"No, I'm a bastard. I wanted to be in your bed. You were great at sex. In the combine? That first time was amazing. I couldn't believe you thought you were bad at it." He kissed her shoulder.

"You did most of the work that day," she whispered.

"Trust me, you did your fare share."

"We have to talk about that day," she said closing her eyes.

Amused at her attempt to hide, he kissed her lips and said, "I'm still here, even when you can't see me."

"I know, but I don't know how you are going to take what I am going to tell you," she said.

"Okay, I'll shut my eyes too."

"We didn't use protection in the combine."

His eyes cracked open, but hers were still tightly closed. "You're right. I never thought about it."

"I am the unluckiest person in the world. The first two times I've had sex, I got pregnant."

"Two?" he whispered and looked at her belly.

"Yes, both times. I am three months along." She took his hand and placed it where his eyes at just been looking.

"My baby. You're having my baby?" he whispered. "We will name him William Hart Reed. We have to get married soon."

Evie smiled at his excitement. Getting pregnant hadn't been in their plan. His bemused smile said he was as excited as she was about the future.

"Once Zoey's wedding is over, we can start planning ours." She laughed.

He pulled her into his arms and kissed her mouth as he said, "We will be married within a week. I am not letting you go again."

"We cannot get married in a week," Evie stated.

"Yes, we will. I cannot take the chance that you will start thinking about it and back out. You have a problem with avoiding me," Jasper said as he kissed her nose.

"I will never avoid you again. I am over that."

"I will not let you avoid me again. Next time I will follow you, yell at you, do whatever it takes to get through that thick skull that I love you." He trailed kisses from her mouth to her neck.

"I love you too, Jasper," Evie said as she pulled his face back to hers so she could kiss his mouth.

EPILOGUE

TRUE TO HIS word six days later, Evie was standing in her wedding dress waiting for her phone's timer to go off. Once it did, Ben would escort her out of the house and up the driveway. She was wearing a long sleeve white dress with a matching shawl. Her shoes were white winter boots. It had snowed the night before so the boots were appropriate.

It had sounded so romantic, getting married on the road between the two farms. At least until it snowed an inch the night before and temperatures ran to just below freezing. Maybe in June it would have been nice, in November, it was cold.

Jasper had wanted to get married where the properties met. Where their lives met. So, the wedding was taking place in the middle of a gravel road.

Ben was looking like a young man in his black suit and tie. He had been excited about Jasper joining the family, and he was not surprised that Evie would have a baby before the school year was out. Since he and Clem had patched up their differences, he had returned to being a happy kid. He had even started talking to his mother again and to Jasper who had moved in the past week.

Both of Evie's sisters were waiting on the couch. Both had been super excited about Evie getting married so quickly, although neither were very excited about the being outdoors in Minnesota in November part. Della had been able to find two matching navy blue jackets that would keep them warm and make nice bridesmaid dresses. They were laughing about something on Zoey's phone, possibly pictures from Gabe of the freezing wedding attendants.

Zoey was happy that Evie was getting married, but was a little miffed the older sister was getting there first. Zoey had been planning her wedding for six months and Evie had hers done in six days. But she was happy her sister was finally happy.

Della didn't say either way if she approved or not, she just jumped into the planning with both feet. Evie had been able to talk to Della about what she had told her as they painted, or at least she had tried to talk to her. Della said she was fine and to forget she ever said anything about it. So, Evie let it drop. But lately she had begun to notice a sadness in her older sister she had never noticed before, a sadness that had been there all along.

The timer went off and Ben silenced it.

"Time to go," Zoey said. Jasper had told them to wait five minutes and then to come out.

The sisters got up from the couch and left the house still laughing as they headed out into the cold. Ben stood at the door until the pair got halfway up the drive, then turned to his mom and offered her his arm. They stepped out into the brisk air and Evie wondered again how the man she loved had talked her into this.

Her breath caught when she saw him standing on the end of the road, waiting for her. There were others waiting also, but she only had eyes for Jasper as they started out down the driveway.

As they walked, Ben said, "Mom, can I ask you a favor?"

She smiled at her son. What were the odds of her son asking her for a favor on her wedding day to the man she asked a favor to?

"Anything, Ben."

"You're changing your name when you marry Jasper, right?" he asked.

"Yes, Ben, but I will always be your mom. Changing my name will not change that." She was starting to worry that she should have talked to her son more about her getting married. Maybe she should have taken more time with her son.

"I know. But you won't be a Singleton anymore. You and Jasper and the baby will all be Reeds. I will be the only one who won't," Ben said.

"Do you want me to see if Jasper will adopt you and you can be a Reed also?" She had thought of it, but hadn't brought it up to Jasper yet. Let him get used to the idea of her and Ben living with him before she asked if he was willing to adopt her son.

Ben's answer surprised her. "I don't want to be a Reed. I like Jasper and everything but I don't want to be a Reed," he explained as they reached the halfway point.

"What do you want?"

"I want to be a Hart. I want to take Grandpa Charley's last name. When I have kids one day, I don't want them to be Singletons. I want them to be Harts." He sounded so grown up talking about the kids he would one day have.

She stopped and hugged her son close to her. Now she was crying, and she had told herself no crying. "Yes, as soon as Della can figure out what needs to be done, you will be Ben Hart."

"I wanted to change it when Grandpa Charley died, but you were a Singleton and I didn't want you to be the only one. But now you are going to be a Reed anyway so I can do it now," he said and Evie's heart broke. She should have changed both their names to Hart years ago. Neither had any loyalty to the Singleton name.

Ben pushed out of her hug and started for the end of the driveway again. She followed and wondered when her son had grown up on her. Touching her growing belly, she wondered if this one would grow up just as fast.

At the end of the driveway, Ben handed her off to Jasper. Pulling her to him, Jasper kissed as he said, "I love you, you look gorgeous."

Chuckling, the minster scolded Jasper. "No kissing until I say you can."

They stopped in front of the minister with the cold wind in their faces. They watched him open his Bible and start with efficient humor. "We are gathered here today in front of all these people who have surely heard these words before. Since it's freezing out: Evangelina Connor Hart Singleton, do you want to marry this guy?"

Evie laughed at his words. "Yes."

Not even waiting for his turn as another gust of cold wind hit them, Jasper laughingly said, "I take Evangelina as my wife."

The minister slammed his Bible shut and said, "You're married!. Kiss her and let's go inside."

By the time Jasper's mouth left Evie's they were alone on the road. The guests were already walking toward Betty's warm house and Evie's loose hair was blowing around them.

"He forgot the ring part," Jasper said into her hair.

"Too cold, I guess." She laughed.

Taking her hand in his, Evie watched him slide a gold ring on her freezing finger. Her gold ring. "Jasper, that's my ring."

"I want you to be able to tell our grandkids that Grandpa loved Grandma so much he let her have her beloved ring back. I added to the engraving though."

Sliding the ring off her freezing finger she looked inside. "You just added a heart."

He took the ring from her hand and slid it back on her finger. "No, I added my heart to it. Now you carry my heart as long as you wear this ring."

Throwing her arms around his neck, she pulled his mouth to hers.

"I am so glad I held your hand during the funeral," she said still trying to control her blowing hair.

"I am glad Grandma made me sit by you because I promise to hold your hand my entire life." He grabbed the hands that were trying to gather her flying hair and kissed the back of them.

"I promise to sit by you every chance I get. Apparently, my hair will be in the way forever." She tried to catch it again.

"I love when your hair is everywhere, it drives me crazy." And he grabbed her face and kissed her and she forgot to control her hair. She was too lost in the kiss and didn't feel the cold wind blowing around them.

ALSO BY ALIE GARNETT

<u>Indulge</u>

Craving Winter

Enticing Aurora

<u>Landstad, ND</u>

Invisible

Irresistible

Impulsive

Insuppressible

Intriguing

Imperfect

Irreplaceable

<u>The Great Lovely Falls</u>

Falling for the Single Mom

Falling for his Best Friends Sister

Falling for the Boss

Falling for his Step-Sister

Falling for his Fake Wife

Falling into a Second Chance

<u>Hart Series</u>

Seeing her Pain

Her Favor

Max Valentine is Looking at Me!

Keeping her Safe

<u>Stand Alone</u>

Romancing the Doctor

CAN'T GET ENOUGH?

How does Della feel about the baby boom after her revelation about her past?

Calls in the middle of the night were never good. Since moving back to Birch Cove, she had started to get used to them. As a lawyer in a small town, she was the first call from jail for drunk drivers or women trying to escape a bad situation. Always in the middle of the night.

The clock red 4 a.m. as she groped for the phone on her nightstand. It never seemed to be where it was supposed to be when it rang.

"Hart & Associates," she stated clearly. Even if it was her personal phone, she answered it as a company phone because calls came in every which way after only a few months back home.

Home, it still didn't feel like it since her return. After living over half her life away from this town, she finally back to stay. So far, she hadn't ventured too far from her work and home, she and didn't feel the need to. People who needed her always seemed to be able to find her.

"Della, it's Gabe," her brother-in-law said in an equally stern voice. He was a cop in town but had never called her in the middle of the night.

"What is it, Gabe?" Her heart in her throat. Was something wrong with her sister? Was there something wrong with the baby that she was carrying?

"Zoey's in labor, and she wanted me to call you," Gabe explained.

"Thank god!" She breathed finally. There was nothing wrong.

"Been waiting for another niece or nephew?" It was an open secret in the family that her sisters were baby crazy, and she was not. But in her defense, she wasn't pregnant—they were.

"Yes, I am," She lied as she always did. Yes, she was happy her sisters were having babies, but no, she did not envy them. Kids were not a part of her life, never had been or were ever going to be. Not anymore.

"Well, come down to the hospital and meet the next one."

"Now or in a few hours? I don't want to have to sit and wait for hours in the middle of the night for this meet and greet."

"Then give it a few hours, but Evie and Jasper are heading over."

"Let them wait. Let me sleep," she grumbled, not wanting to spend hours in the same room as Evie with nothing to do but wait. "Thanks, Gabe. I will be down there soon."

Two hours later, after she had leisurely showered and dressed for her day, she headed out the hospital to see her new niece or nephew. Zoey and Gabe opted to not find out which they were having, unlike Evie, who had wanted to know instantly so she could plan.

Evie had called as she was getting out of the shower that the baby was there, so there would be no waiting for Della. Nothing more, not a single detail, since Della wasn't there. Not that Della cared one way or another; she would love either one equally. Though she knew Evie wanted a girl from Zoey just like she had a few weeks before.

Walking into the hospital room, she nearly walked right back out. Both her sisters were snuggling a blanket that she was sure contained a baby. Each had a husband who was right there, looking at their wife and baby with so much love Della could barely handle it.

"Hey, new mommy," she said to her sister and held up a brightly wrapped package. Yes, it was a defensive move, and she knew it. She just hoped her sister didn't.

"Della, you came." Zoey barely looked up from the baby as she said it.

"Did you think I wouldn't? Do I have a new niece?"

"Nephew." Gabe smiled.

"Another one of those. Congratulations, guys." Della handed the package to Gabe. It was the exact same thing she had given Evie and Jasper a month before when Willow was born. Having to find something new and unique when they were coming every month had been impossible.

"Thanks, Della. His name is Connor Gabriel."

"Really?" She laughed, though she was actually surprised that the baby's middle name wasn't Hart like his cousin Willow's. And now her older nephew's last name was Hart, thanks to her.

"Did you want to hold him?" Zoey asked, lifting the blankets her way a little.

"Not today. Kind of not feeling well right now. This weekend for sure." She lied again. So far, she hadn't held Willow and had no plans to do so anytime in the future.

"Keep your sickness on that side of the room." Zoey kidded as she continued to look at the baby.

"I really have to head back to the office. Big case to get ready for. Congratulations again." She lied and backed out of the room slowly.

"You're coming out when I get out of the hospital, right?" Zoey sounded nervous, and Della hoped that Evie would be there for her because Della didn't know anything about babies.

"Yes, just call me when they spring you." She joked, hoping to lighten the mood.

"I will."

Della headed out the door and hurried down the hall as fast as her heels could take her, which was fast because she always wore heels. Pushing out of the hospital, she sucked in a deep breath of chilly morning air as she counted to ten. Then did it again.

It was even harder than she had imagined it would be, and it was only going to get worse because these babies were going nowhere. Her sisters were lucky on that count, and on every other count there was.

Shaking off the old feelings of missing out, she headed for her car to go back to work. It was all she had, after all. Work.

Is there anything that can take Della's mind off work?

ABOUT ALIE GARNETT

I love to read and prefer a little spice in those books. I am lucky enough to live on a small hobby farm in northern Minnesota with her husband and two kids. I enjoy spending time in the pasture with my two mini horses and one fainting goat (who doesn't actually faint). When I'm not writing, I'm busy trying to do all the things I didn't get to while writing. Or maybe I wouldn't have gotten to them anyway, because its laundry, dishes and fun things like that.